# A GODD\*MNED

# Christmas Miracle

BY

SPARKLE HAYTER

### PUBLISHER'S NOTE

This is a work of fiction. Names, characters, places, and incidents either are the product of the author's imagination or are used fictitiously, and any resemblance to actual persons, living or dead, events, or locales is entirely coincidental.

For the gang

# TABLE OF CONTENTS

# DECEMBER 22ND

# 1

# MOUSE COMES HOME

Irma makes the best strudel, everyone agrees. She puts an old tablecloth on the yellow formica table, a sunshine yellow table that reminds her of the one her parents had on the farm in Saskatchewan, and she rolls the ball of strudel dough on top of it, first with a rolling pin, then with her hands, patting it carefully until the dough is stretched over the whole table, so thin you can read the newspaper through it. Then she brushes it with melted butter, gently so it doesn't tear. She puts lots of butter into the apple filling too, along with a generous dose of cinnamon, brown sugar, and secret ingredients (cumin and a hint of white pepper). The way she makes it, the pastry is flaky and the filling is moist and lightly caramelized with a light spicy bite. In 1985, it won a prize at the Pioneer Days fair and you can still see the plaque on top of the television, behind the clutter of family photos in pewter and hammered tin frames.

After it is filled, rolled, and the top scored, she puts it in the fridge to harden the butter so it won't melt too quickly in the hot oven and the layers of dough will puff up when it bakes.

Gord is awakened at 3 a.m. by the soft thump of a rolling pin on dough. A siren screaming down the street won't rouse him, but the whispery sounds of Irma in the kitchen after midnight always do. She used to do this all the time, it's a way for her to work off anxiety, and she'd waved off Gord's concern with a simple, "I'm a farm girl, I can handle it." But when Gord pointed out that her parents had died in their 50s, he got her to take it a little easier, to "hit the hay" at a decent hour and get at least seven hours sleep before she went to her job at the glass company.

This is a special occasion, and she has the next day off work. Gord rolls over and goes back to sleep.

"I want Mouse to know I fussed," she says to Gord the next morning, as she reaches for the phone. The strudel is in the oven now and the house warm and atmospheric with the smells of hot butter and apples and yeast.

"Who ya callin'?"

"Whiskey."

When Whiskey answers, she says, "Changed your mind yet?"

Whiskey brays back loudly, "If Mouse was the last guy on earth I wouldn't cross the street to spit on him! I wouldn't piss on that jackass if he was on fire— "

"Whiskey, he's been gone a long time. Hard time. And it's Christmas, eh?"

"Irma, he burned me three times. He busted my television, he owes me money, and he stole Tammy. Three strikes and you're out. You call me when he's not there, and I'll bring over your presents. But if he's there, I'm going to kick his ass to fucking CHINA!"

He hangs up without saying good-bye.

"Merry fuckin' Christmas to you too, you shithead," she says to the dial tone, before hanging up the phone hard.

3

She turns to Gord. "I don't think Whiskey's gonna change his mind."

"He's just full of the milk of human kindness."

"It's been seven fucking years."

"He's still hurtin' over Tammy."

"It's not just Tammy. He's still raw about the time Mouse tried to fix his TV and broke it. Whiskey's no saint, eh. Jesus H, he's not mad at Darryl for taking Tammy, is he? Only Mouse."

"You know Whiskey."

"Well, he should be thankful to Mouse for saving him. It coulda been Whiskey in jail if he'd stayed with Tammy. And now I have to keep these two apart. It fucks everything up, Gord. Jesus fucking Christ, and I don't have enough to worry about with Mouse—"

"Irma, I have a system, I'll put a cigar in the lawn Santa's mouth and tell Whiskey not to come in if he sees the stogie."

"Okay, but it still ruins the reconciliation if Whiskey won't reconcile. That asshole."

# 2

# PRESIDENT OF POLAND

Mouse had flown on a plane just twice, once when he was sent out to Elk Woods federal penitentiary, and once when he was flown back to Wesaskawa. On the first flight he was in handcuffs and accompanied by other prisoners like him and the men guarding them, and, on his return, in economy class, in a suit like a regular person. It's whole different world. The flight attendants smile at him and he feels happy and normal. This is how he wants to stay for the rest of his life.

An old guy trades seats with him so Mouse can sit by the window, like a child, looking down at the wide, unfenced country below. He's delighted like a child with the airplane meal too, though he says later the food was better in prison.

Some of his old friends are waiting at the airport with a sign that says, "Welcome Brent Kuszynski, President of Poland." Irma holds the sign, but the lettering is in Gord's hand. Though people around them strain to see who the president of Poland is, the joke is lost on Brent "Mouse" Kuszynski. He just wants to cry, because his old friends are here, the good friends, the ones he thought he'd lost because of the crack. He figured Irma would be there; she'd sent him letters and care packages every month while he was in jail, cookies, books, and Chinese

5

sandalwood soap he liked, and Gord because Gord was her husband and a forgiving type. But Lisa is there, a little older but still sharp in her black leather Harley jacket and jeans, and Norm is there, a big redheaded gent who grins at him. Whiskey, Ginger, Glenn, Darryl and, yeah, Tammy are missing, but his oldest and best friends are all there, and just as Dr. Lobo, the prison psychiatrist, suggested, he looks on the bright side.

"Welcome home," Irma says, and hugs him. Then they all hug him, hard, until he bursts into tears.

"This guy needs a beer," Gord says.

On the drive from the airport Mouse can't take his eyes off the expanse of limitless prairie whizzing by on both sides of the highway, seamless and white with a fresh dusting of snow. It excites him at first, but then makes him uncomfortable. By the time they get to town, he's had enough and is happy when he gets into the close coziness of Gord and Irma's cluttered house.

Irma puts his bag in the spare room. The room has red and yellow walls, green curtains and a bright blue bedspread.

"I feel like I'm in a box of crayons, Irma," he says.

"Gord painted it specially for you."

"I love you guys." Mouse bursts into tears again.

"We love you too, Mouse. I got something for ya." She takes a manila envelope out of her purse. "We got together one night and—I won't lie, most of us were pretty pissed off with you for a while. Then Lisa remembered the time you fixed up that old car for her so she could drive to work. And I said, you know we'd all be going to jail if things had worked out different, if we'd been caught in one of our many crimes. So we all told stories about you, nice stories about all the good things you did for us, and everyone kicked in some money."

"I can't take your money."

"Yes you can. When Gord and I were both out of work in '95 and '96 and you came over with groceries and beer every Friday? Well, now we're both working and we can pay for those groceries."

"You don't have to—"

"Yes we do, Mouse. So we're square, eh?"

"We're more than square."

"Don't cry, Mouse. Don't cry. Now I gotta tell ya. Whiskey's still pissed off and he's avoiding ya. And he didn't kick in any money. After all those times you took him for his chemo! He's a fuckhead but you know Whiskey. So Gord's devised a system with the lawn Santa. He'll tell you," she says. "Something else. Beer and a joint, that's all now, eh Mouse? No more crack or trash like that."

"No, I'm clean now, Irma. No crack, nothing, not even a drop of beer, eh? I could use a near-beer now though."

"Okay, but just near-beer and pot, and only on weekends and holidays or I'm driving you to rehab myself."

"Yeah, I'm cool with that."

"You know I'll kick your ass if you go stupid again—cuz you're a smart guy Mouse, and a good one. You wanna take a shower?"

"Do I smell bad?"

Irma sniffs him. "No, nice. That aftershave?"

"Yeah, I made it myself in kitchen workshop. It's cinnamon, nutmeg, and cloves."

"You smell like Christmas, Mouse."

He follows her downstairs to the rec room, which he notices with satisfaction hasn't changed much. There are more gewgaws, but they have the same black furniture covered with the same crocheted afghans in red and green that Irma put over them every Christmas. They have the same red and brown rug, the same Oilers memorabilia, the same marijuana leaf coffee cups, the larger collection of German-looking beer steins. The tree in the corner has the same ornaments.

And there is a sign, hand-lettered with gold glitter paint, held aloft by a piece of gold tinsel strung diagonally across the ceiling: "Welcome Home Mouse."

He starts to cry again.

"Turn off the waterworks," Lisa says. "You'll dehydrate. Jesus. Guy needs a beer." She gives him a hug. "Welcome home, Mousie."

✳✳✳

"Prison wasn't so bad, once I got used to it. Had my own cell with a television and a desk. I got my GED in there."

"No shit?" Norm says.

"No shit. But I'm glad to be out."

"You had a TV?" Irma asks. "Did you have satellite?"

"Yeah, but most of the channels was blocked. We got CBC, CTV, Global, Newsworld, the Aboriginal channel, an educational channel and the French CBC thing," he said. "They give us TV so's when we get out, we're not like 'Rip Van Winkle, lost in a new world.'"

"Did you have a toilet and a shower?" Gord asks.

"I had a toilet and a sink. I got to shower alone but a lot of times, I'd just fill a little bucket with water and stand over the toilet and pour the water on me. Then I'd have ta mop it up, eh?"

"So you had a mop."

"I had ta ask for the mop. Guard brought it and watched me and took it back when I was done, so's I couldn't turn it into a weapon."

"Did ya have friends in there?"

"Yeah, not friends like you, but there was a guy I played cards with, Joe Bakie. He was in for stealing a truck full of stuff being delivered to the Rexall. He was so desperate, he tried to sell two crates of tampons to buy crack."

Now, Norm cries. "Man, it's good to have you home, Mouse."

Mouse looks around at everyone, looking at him, smiling at him, echoing Norm—yeah, good to have you home, Mouse. After everything that happened, they're happy to see me, he thinks, with amazement.

And then the tears again. Mouse cried on a dime. Everyone had worried about him going to jail, how he'd survive, being such a softy, so sentimental, and a little guy to boot. But here he was, and he seemed better than ever. He was off crack, and he said he had a life plan now, a better plan than, "rob a 7-11 to get money to open a nail salon for my wife Tammy."

"What're you gonna do now, Mousie?"

"Try to get a job at my uncle Murph's junkyard, once I get up the stones to call the sonvabitch."

"We can invite Murph to Christmas Eve, Mouse. Might make it easier if other people are around," says Irma.

"You seen Tam?" he asks.

"She fucked off to BC," Lisa says.

"You got her number?"

"You don't want to see her," Irma says. "She's with some other... guy."

"Oh," he says and looks at his feet. "Where's Lorne?"

"He's in the Northwest Territories, eh, working in the diamond mines," Norm answers. "Way the fuck up at Snap Lake."

"The mine is 500 hectares, underground, they gotta whole world down there, movie theater, gym, cafeteria. He makes a shitload of money. He's got a girl in Yellowknife, and he's spendin' Christmas with her 'n her family," Gord adds.

"And Darryl?"

The doorbell rings.

"Pizza's here," Gord says.

It isn't pizza. It's Sherry, Norm's wife, whom he'd met while he was in the hospital for his appendix. A six foot black nurse, built like an Amazon, heart of gold, Norm says. She's still in her uniform.

"Anyone gonna get me a beer," she asks.

"You sit, sweetie, I'll get ya a beer. She's been on her feet all day, looking after people."

"See why I married this guy?"

"So I got a system with the lawn Santa," Gord says. "If the cigar is in the lawn Santa's mouth, Whiskey won't come in. No cigar, Whiskey's here."

"No cigar and I'll stay outside too," Lisa fumes. "That bigot Whiskey. V'you seen his Christmas lights? The whole fucking house is covered in lights, eh? All the trees in the yard. It's blinding."

Gord agrees. "You think ya died and you're heading to the white light."

"I said to him, Whiskey, aren't you worried about wasting energy and the environment?"

"And the electric bill," Irma adds.

"And he says, he does it to piss off the Shi'ites because they hate Christmas. I said, Whiskey, you gotta lot of Shi'ites in your neighborhood, do ya? And he says, there's some. Turns out, they're Indian, Sikhs I think. Jesus. Whiskey's what happens when stupid people get a lot of money." Lisa shakes her head.

"He's got his good points," Gord says.

"He's gotten worse since he won the lottery."

"Whiskey won the lottery?" Mouse says.

"He won a hundred grand plus, a second prize, not the big one, Mousie."

"Hey, a toast." Gord raises his elaborate commemorative beer stein from Oktoberfest in Munchner, Alberta 1987. "To Mouse. And to friends. Times without money are better than times without pot, and times without pot and money are better than times without friends. But these are the best times, we got money, we got pot, and we got our friends."

When the pizza comes, they eat it properly, off china plates with side salad, and catch Mouse up on everyone. Gord is still in the oil patch, up to 20 days a month in the field laying pipeline now oil prices are high, the rest at home. Irma has a new job cutting glass at Glassco. She measures the glass, she cuts it, she wraps it up in corrugated cardboard. Norm is now a foreman in ceramics at Glassco, where the boss's daughter Patricia Winter was instituting new things like time clocks and generally making everyone's life harder. Once a month or so he and Gord drive down to Edmonton to see the Oilers or the Eskimos play—they'd gone in with some other guys and bought season tickets. Since Mouse had been gone, Lisa had married, had two boys, and divorced, and was being stalked by her ex-husband's ex-girlfriend, who was, unluckily, a cop. Lisa had quit Glassco when the union was busted and was cutting hair in her cousin Wanda's beauty salon.

Sherry had come into the group with Norm six months before and felt right at home, though she is still new and in a phase of listening and not talking much. Everyone else talks more than enough to make up for her, she says. Sherry is Norm's third wife, but he was one of those people who learn from their mistakes and he was doing really well in this marriage, everyone agrees. When Gord passes around a fatty, Norm abstains because he's driving, and only drinks one near-beer. Normally, he'd have a Labatt's, but he feels like he has to set a good example for Mouse.

When Mouse reaches for his third piece of pizza, Irma notices that he's lost the top of his left pinky.

"What happened!" She grabs his hand. "Were you in a fight?"

"Rat chewed it off."

"No fucking way!"

"I'm shittin' ya."

"What really happened?"

"This guy, eh? On the way to prison. He told everyone on the prison bus they had to call him Mr. Frank Sinatra, then he bit off the tip of my finger."

Irma: "Jesus Fucking Christ."

"Hurt like a sonvabitch. They tried to sew it back on in the prison hospital but the wound was too ragged. I spent my first week in prison in the hospital all doped up."

Lisa: "He sounds mental."

"Nah. He wasn't nuts, just scared of prison. Someone told him to act crazy, like big cray eh, so's the mean guys would steer clear of him in the joint and he'd get his own cell. Joke was on him though cuz everyone gets their own cell in the Woods."

Norm: "Joke was on him? You lost the tip of your finger!"

Mouse shrugs and changes the subject to their larger circle of friends and relatives and they talk about Goofy, Fat Pat, Rupee, Estelle, Critter, and others until Norm stands up and says, "We have to go pick up Sherry's kid from her Mom and Dad's. Stay cool, Mouse. We'll see you Christmas Eve."

The landline in the kitchen rings and Irma follows Norm and Sherry upstairs, the voices muting as she closes the kitchen door.

"Merry Christmas," Irma says into the phone.

A man answers. "Yeah, you too, eh? Can I speak to uh, Brent?"

"Who's calling?"

"It's a friend of his Dad."

Irma knows better. Mouse's dad, dead ten years, never had a friend.

"Let me see if I can find him," she says, staying right where she is but moving the speaker away from her mouth so the other party can't hear her breathing.

She hears the guy say, "Getting him," and a woman say, "Thanks, buddy. Here's your tenner." It's Tammy. Fucking Tammy. Irma puts her hand over the phone and says in a deeper voice, "Hello?"

"Mouse? Is that you? Oh God, Baby, I've missed you. How are you?"

"It's Irma, Tammy. Stay away from Mouse."

"I'm still his wife. You can't tell me that."

"Yes, I can."

It's Christmas and Irma would really like to be a good Christian, all understanding and sympathy. Bad things happened to Tammy to make her this way. Both her parents had died when Tammy was young and she'd been shunted around foster homes until she ran away from foster care with her best friend Cindy Crowchild. There'd been drugs, petty crime, and bad men—Cindy had been murdered by a man they'd worked with, and many others had OD'd.

But all Irma can think of is Mouse, already terrified on the prison bus when some shit stick bit off his pinky finger in order to get his own cell. What else had happened to Mouse that he hadn't told her about in his letters from Elk Woods? It's a strain to keep her imagination in check, but impossible to hold her temper. Mouse took the whole rap and Tammy didn't have to spend a single day in jail.

"Stay in BC, Tam, because if you set foot in Wesaskawa—hell, if you set foot anywhere in Alberta, I will track you like a bloodhound and punch you till you're ugly. You stay away from Mouse."

"Don't write checks your ass can't cash, Irma," Tammy says, hanging up so she gets the last word.

Irma figures Tammy and Darryl have split, and now she's broke and looking for a sucker. She sits down at the yellow formica table and takes a cigarette from the blue and white pack of Player's Navy Cut that Gord left there, lighting it with a Christmas match and inhaling deeply. Six months ago, she quit smoking, but she doesn't care. If she doesn't smoke this cigarette she's going to collapse in tears, and it's Christmas, a time to be joyful and full of goodwill towards men and all that.

The tears come anyway but she blinks them back, distracting herself by studying the picture on the Player's pack, a bearded sailor framed in a life preserver with two 19th century sailing ships behind him. Irma's father smoked Player's, hand-rolleds made from a tin of loose tobacco, but every Christmas Irma's mom got him a square tin of fat pre-rolled cigarettes. Those cigarettes he rationed, saving them for the bad days. She never saw her father cry, no matter what disaster befell them. Instead of crying, he went to the tin of rolled cigarettes, lit one and puffed away, staring at the sky. They lived some years on carrot stew and homemade noodles boiled in milk, and they survived and went on. All seven kids became smokers.

She's so upset, she doesn't think to look at the number in the phone's small LED screen, from area code 587, although if she had, it might not have rung any bells anyway, since 587 had only recently gone into circulation. If she had noticed, and if it had rung any bells, she would have realized that Tammy was already in Alberta.

After her cigarette, Irma puts in some eye drops, checks herself in the round mirror magnet on the fridge to make sure she doesn't look like she's been crying and goes back downstairs, pausing in the back porch landing for a deep breath and a deep exhalation before returning to the party.

"Honey, where's that DVD we made for Mouse? Mouse, we got a lotta photos put on a DVD for you," Gord says.

Irma takes the DVD from under the Christmas tree and hands it to him. He pulls it from its red-and-white striped cardboard Christmas sleeve and slides it into the player. The lights go down.

Irma thinks she'll go back upstairs, bring down the coffee and the strudel. But Mouse falls asleep about five minutes later, in a big armchair so cushiony and soft it feels like a hug. It's been a long day and a long seven years.

# DECEMBER 23RD

# 3

# WHAT KIND OF ASSHOLE CHRISTIAN DOESN'T BELIEVE IN CHRISTMAS?

Ginger wonders, as she peeks in the windows of her ex-husband's house. No Christmas tree, no gifts, nothing festive at all in this severe home, just beige walls, navy blue furniture, and a big crucifix over the fireplace with a Jesus who looks like an Allman brother going through withdrawal. Was shitty decor some kind of Christian virtue in the New Church of the Lamb of God, or as Ginger calls it, New CLOG?

It's bad enough Leo had to skip Halloween, a "celebration of Satan," but no Christmas? Jesus H. Christ—no pun intended, a kid waits all year for Christmas, and a year is a long time when you're a child. And the judge thinks Randy is a better parent? Unfuckingbelievable. Okay, sure, Randy had given up his porn and his cocaine, but what kind of shame-filled bullshit life was this for a kid?

"Christmas a pagan rite disguised as a Christian holy day," Randy said when he'd called to tell her Leo wasn't coming. He was parroting his pastor. "Jesus was born in June, and it's an occasion for reverence not for gluttony and beer pong—"

"It's a day for family and friends to get together, to eat, drink, and be merry in the spirit of Jesus, who himself would not give a flying fuck what day we celebrate."

Randy sighed his "condescending convert" sigh, a term Lisa came up with for born-agains and cleaned up drunks who, once they converted/rehabbed, lorded it over those who hadn't.

"Leo has strep. He can't travel. I have a court order, Ginger."

Fuck your court order, Randy, Ginger thinks now, as she watches Linda enter the living room. Ginger pulls herself back into a snowy bush, hiding but still able to see Linda from this side angle. The new Mrs. Randy LaFontaine is thin and drawn. Around her neck hangs a heavy crucifix, a smaller, mobile version of the one over the fireplace. Goddamn, Ginger thinks, Jesus is suffering and dying in every room this woman walks into.

Ginger's phone rings with a few key chords from Pink Floyd's Shine on You Crazy Diamond, and she jerks back with a start. The bushes rustle. Linda hears it and turns but doesn't see Ginger, who vanishes around the house. The snow is fresh and soft. It doesn't crunch, instead absorbing the sound of her boots.

Behind the garage, she checks her phone; it's an alarm reminding her to call Irma. She turns it off and sneaks back to the window.

Maybe ten kilometers from here, Randy is at work bulldozing trees in Black Pines, and won't be home until after six. For a day, Ginger's been casing the house from a safe distance, her only disguise her normal winter wear, which covers her from head to toe—except for her eyes. Today is the first day she's gone close enough to peek in. Today is the day she'll act, one way or another.

Linda looks around the room, searching for something, and finds it, a book, on a brown end table that looks like crap particle board painted to look like wood. Ginger's eyes follow her out of the room, then she moves around the house until she sees Linda in the kitchen, standing over Leo, who writes in a paper notebook. The sight of Leo makes Ginger's heart feel like it's collapsing in on itself and bursting at the same time.

Linda home schools him. All things considered, Leo looks good, hale and hearty though a little pale, and not like a kid struck down by strep. She knew it, Randy cooked this up to keep Leo from her because it's too hard to brainwash Leo when he has to compete with Ginger and Christmas, especially the way she did it up.

When a timer on the table goes off, Leo closes the book, and Linda walks to the fridge, extracting a pot, then to the stove to heat it up, her back to the window. This emboldens Ginger, who moves in to the window to get a better look at Leo.

Maybe it's a coincidence, or maybe it's the bond between Mother and Son that makes Leo sense her presence and look at her. He smiles and his whole face lights up. She smiles back and winks, nods her head towards the back of the house. He winks back and says to Linda, "May I be excused to go to the washroom?" Ginger doesn't hear Linda's response as Linda is a soft-talker, but she sees Leo get up and leave the kitchen.

The back door has a tense spring and snaps shut with a bang. Linda's head jerks around. Ginger beats a fast retreat, grabbing Leo by the hand while pressing the auto-start button on her car's remote control with the other. The car, which is covered in streaky mud everywhere but the windows, is parked down the alley behind a stand of big pine trees. It's still cold when they get there, but the back window and front windshield are starting to clear of frost, enough that Ginger can see

Linda running down the back alley in the rear view mirror. Linda's mouth is wide open like she's shouting but Ginger can't hear any words. She guns the engine, and squeals out, leaving Linda in a cloud of grey exhaust and white condensation.

"She'll have your license plate number," Leo says.

"Fake plates and a fake BMW logo," Ginger says.

As soon as she's sure Linda hasn't picked up her trail, Ginger pulls over to the shoulder and stops.

"Open your mouth, Leo." She peers down his throat. "You don't have strep, do you?"

"No."

"Aren't sick at all, are you?"

"No."

"I knew it. And you're taller."

"I had a growth spurt," Leo says. "I'm glad you kidnapped me."

"It's not really a kidnapping, Leo. I mean, I was supposed to get you for the holidays, and then Randy got the court to keep you with him because he lied about your sore throat. Did he forge that doctor's letter?"

"I saw a doctor. He belongs to our church."

"THEIR church, Leo. We're Anglican."

Ginger pulls back onto the highway, heading west instead of east because she figures if Linda sets the cops on her they'll look for her heading east towards Alberta. This will buy her time to get to the Robowash to remove the mud on the car, revealing its true blue-black color, then drive around the back where the vacuums were, not to vacuum, but for privacy so she can pry off the fake BMW logo, along with the fake plates, and the fake decal that reads: "Winter-Masciuk Elite BMW Dealers," taken off the near-totalled car of one of the Winter family brats who crashed it after prom, injuring three.

She lets Leo help her attach a second set of fake license plates, Saskatchewan plates.

"Are you hungry?" she says to Leo. "Wanna stop somewhere for a bite?"

"No. Can we keep driving til we get to Uncle Andy's?"

They head to Andy Why's place near Squilax, BC, through a roundabout route of back roads. Andy runs a marijuana grow op there, and one of their best customers is a doctor who will examine Leo there. This isn't going to be like all those times Ginger flew by the seat of her lacy underpants. This time, she had a plan, a burner phone she bought off a Somali guy in The Klondiker, which she charged up using a website for an Egyptian cell provider, along with fake plates and logos, and a map she'd gone over and over to determine the safest, most discreet route.

"Sure. Take my phone, call your Auntie Irma and tell her we're coming for Christmas. Then find us a radio station."

# 4

# THE FIRST GIRL WE MET IN A DUMPSTER

"You were twelve before you had your first Canadian Christmas?" Norm says, in the car, driving Sherry to work the next day.

It's still dark at this early hour, 7 a.m., and on moonless nights the landscape is a silhouette of black and grey shadows. But there is a moon, and a big snowfall overnight has turned this part of the country, where the prairie turns hilly, into a glittery Christmas card, all the industrial, rusty, and ugly now covered in a thick undulating blanket that catches the morning moonlight with a million tiny sparks of light.

"When I was an infant we stayed here but I don't remember that," Sherry says. By now the heater has completely cleared the frost from the windows, but it's still cold enough inside the car to encase their words in white clouds of condensed frozen breath, like comic strip balloons. "Every year after that until I was 12 we went to Jamaica to see family."

"Cool. Was it like the thing we're going to Christmas Day at the Caribbean Center, Grand Market?"

"GRAN' Market. A bit. It was wonderful, but, I was a kid, a part of me wanted to do what all the other kids were doing for Christmas. When

Dad became district school superintendent and moved my grandparents up here we began staying for Christmas and going to Jamaica for the new year."

"Tell me your first memory of Jamaica Christmas."

"Well, it involves Canada. I wanted to bring some snow to my grandmothers who had never seen it in real life. I was three, and didn't understand that snow melts. I secretly put some in a little jar and hid it in my suitcase."

"And you took it out and it was water."

"Yes, and I was so disappointed. My mother found it when we got to Jamaica. She froze it in my grandma's freezer, and then took it to a man who made snow-cones, and he turned it back into snow for us."

"So you had Canadian snow in Jamaica for Christmas."

"It wasn't the same though, because now it was just granules, not individual snowflakes. It was a jar of broken snowflakes."

"Aw."

"But my grandmothers loved it."

"Tell me again what we'll eat at GRAN' market?"

"Jerk chicken, seafood patties, oxtail stew, black cake, fruit salad—"

Norm's phone rings. It's Irma. He puts it on speaker.

"Irma!"

"Tammy called last night looking for Mouse. I told her fuck right off, more or less, but I'm worried she's heading our way to reconnect with Mouse."

"Shit. Well, Eddie Redfeather might have Darryl's contact info."

"Okay, thanks Norm. See you later." Click.

"Who is Tammy?" Sherry says.

"Tammy's the girl who messed Mouse up, and the first girl we met in a dumpster."

"You met more than one girl in a dumpster?"

"Yeah, it's a whole story. That's the same night we learned that drain cleaner won't eat through a pot plant."

"Start from the beginning."

"Okay, it was 1987. We all had mullets. Yeah, Gord's got some photos somewhere, all of us in mullets, Whiskey, Glenn, Mouse, Gord, Darryl, Mel, Eddie, and me. Anyway, Whiskey was living in the Glendale Arms, 7th floor. We were makin' this big dope deal with these three gents from Edmonton, big motherfuckers. We'd just paid 'em and the intercom buzzes.

"It's like after midnight, 1 or 2 a.m. Mouse answers it and hears, 'Police, please let us in.' Darryl looks out the window and sure enough, there's cops at the front door. Big scary sonvabitches, eh. Back then cops looked like cops, six feet tall, barrel-chested guys. We've got dope all over the table, posters of pot leaves, and this pot plant Mouse grew. Air's full of pot smoke, like, you can see the haze. But Mouse has no choice, eh? So he buzzes them in.

"Lucky for us, the elevator's busted and the cops have to walk up six flights. The three Edmonton guys take their money and leave down the emergency stairs, and we start cleaning the place up. Mouse scoops up the pot in a black garbage bag and takes it to the old lady next door to hide in her oven.

"We open the windows and take down the posters. Gord pulls the pot plant out by its roots and stuffs it down the toilet. Only, it won't go down, and it won't come out. Gord stuffs it in as far as he can, and then he pulls down his pants and sits on top of it, like he's on the toilet, eh? So if the cops open the door they'll just think he's taking a shit."

Sherry laughs so hard she tears up.

"We're waving the pot smoke out the windows with newspapers, waitin' for the cops. And they don't come. And they don't come. We wait, like, an hour. Scared shitless. Stoned out of our gourds. Big red eyes. Finally, we hear the doorbell. Mouse answers and two cops are there. You can just tell from the way they look at us they know we're all fogged to toons. They ask Whiskey some questions about a guy upstairs. Turns out the neighbor filed a complaint because the guy threatened to beat him with a skillet so they came to check it out, and they don't care about the weed.

"Meanwhile, Gord's still sitting on the john. When the cops leave, we try to get that fucking pot plant out of the toilet again but we can't. So Gord hatches this plan, we'll go to the 7-11 and buy a bunch of drain opener, the corrosive stuff. We'll use that to dissolve the pot plant.

"We're walking to the 7-11, the one up on Highway 11, eh, and we hear this woman's voice, and it sounds like it's coming from the Kentucky Fried dumpster. I'm the biggest 'n tallest and I'm elected to go in and get her out. She's drunk as a skunk, so it's a harder job than ya think. I pick her up and she flops like a rag doll, legs everywhere, but I finally get her hoisted over the top and the guys help her down.

"She's just 18, name's Tammy, she was out drinking with some friends so-called who got pissed off at her and threw her into the dumpster. After that she's all over me for a while because I went into the dumpster and I'm her big hero. I told her I was seein' someone. I was too, Frankie.'

"So Gord and I go to work on the pot plant in the toilet, but the drain cleaner doesn't do a damn thing, eh. We ended up getting Frankie's brother, he's a plumber, to come in and fix it, and paid him with pot."

"From the black garbage bag Mouse put in the old lady's oven."

"Yeah, cool old lady. Mrs. Dronyk. We paid her with pot too. Anyways, this girl, Tammy, she smells like grease and fried chicken and Whiskey says, 'you smell good enough to eat,' then she's all over him. They're together—well, off and on—for like ten years.

"We kinda put up with her because Whiskey loved her, and she told a good story. But she and Whiskey fought like starving dogs. Man. One time at the Klondiker he said something she didn't like and she overturned a whole table full of beer and went at him. Big drinker. And then she started doing coke a lot, eh, but trying to hide it from us. We gotta rule, no powders no needles no guns. Even when we were doin' banks, we didn't use guns."

"Did Mouse rob banks with you?"

"Nah. He only did petty crimes, like selling some pot, until Tammy."

"You guys are lucky you didn't all go to prison."

"Charged once, no conviction." Norm grins, a little too proud of this in her opinion.

"Anyway, when Tammy started doing crack, Whiskey got fed up and tried to get her into rehab but she took off, and moved in with Mouse. Mouse kept Tammy a secret for a while. They'd come to parties or to the bar separately so Whiskey didn't know for the longest time. When he found out he was burned that Mouse took up with her."

"She sounds awful. What did Mouse see in her?"

"She's pretty, kinda. Mouse just couldn't believe such a pretty girl loved him. He hasn't had a lotta girlfriends, he's shy with women. Low self-esteem you know?"

"He seems like a nice guy."

"He is. Real nice. He wouldn't hurt a fly but the crack and the woman, you know, did a number on him. He started doing crack too so he could share something with her, something she enjoyed, the way you got me golfing—different, but the same motive. They got married. Before long he had no money left, and he robbed a 7-11 with a loaded sawed-off, so he got seven years because second offense, pot bust in 1995, and a shit lawyer. All for Tammy. She played him like a cheap guitar."

"And now Tammy has gone off with some other guy."

"She ran off with Darryl. Don't say anything. We gotta break it to Mouse quiet. He and Darryl used to be real close. The story we agreed on is that Darryl took off with some crazy bitch, so it's not a lie. We don't wanna lie to him, eh."

"You guys are so sweet," Sherry says. "Not for one moment do I regret marrying you."

"Yeah, well, why would ya?" he says, and grins, still oblivious to the fact that her parents are very upset about her and Norm, whom they refer to as "that white boy with the ninth grade education."

Her parents' objections were also, and she hates to admit this, aesthetic. Her mother, especially, just didn't like the way Sherry and Norm looked together, Norm a big flaming redhead, white like a vampire or Julian Assange, 6 foot 4. Even if they weren't an interracial couple, they would be drawing stares. Oddly, Sherry doesn't mind the extra attention Norm gets, because it makes it a bit more of a shared burden. Norm doesn't go out of his way to avoid attention either. Sometimes, walking down the street, he'd just stop and look up, and because he was so tall, everyone else noticed and did the same. While they were all looking up, Norm would look down and slip away with Sherry unnoticed.

Funny, but there wasn't anything Sherry particularly liked about Norm when she first met him, but after three weeks she broke off her engagement to the guy who owned the Big Man shop in Centennial Mall. Four months after that, she and Norm got married in the Elvis church in Vegas.

Sherry's parents didn't approve of the wedding or anything about Norm except his high wages and fiscal responsibility, but they never liked the guy from the Big Man Shop either. They liked her ex-husband, the doctor, for God's sake.

"What about the other woman you found in a dumpster?"

"Oh, yeah, a stripper named Twyla," Norm said. "Some guys threw her in after a bachelor party. Fuckers. Gord and I heard her, fished her out, let her take a shower at Gord's place, made her some tea. Never saw her again."

"You're the Dumpster angels. She's lucky it was you guys who found her."

"I guess. There are a lotta shitty people in the world."

# 5

# EXPERIENCE! SAVOR! APPRECIATE!

SMILEY O'REILLY (energetic and cheerful): Good Morning, from CNJK Radio, broadcasting from Nojack, the heart of Wesaskawa County, home of Glassco Glass and Metalworks, and the Centennial Cup champs, The Wesaskawa Tigers.

(canned cheer: Goooo Tigers!)

I'm Smiley O'Reilly taking the baton from your night man, Moonlight Marvin Pysenko. G'Night Marvin.

MARVIN: (His voice distant and tired, a sharp contrast to SMILEY) Yeah. Night.

SMILEY: It's Wednesday morning and it's delivery day at Glassco, so you might want to steer clear of the Aberhart highway until 10 a.m. It's going to be a warm and sunny today. Roger the Rainman will be here with a complete forecast on the half hour. Hey Roger, did you hear about the guy who bought the underground storage room of the bank?

ROGER (in a voice completely devoid of enthusiasm, or any other emotion): No.

SMILEY: People complained that it was all his vault. Ha ha.

When Mouse wakes up the next morning, he wakes up feeling that same heavy feeling, the "rock on my chest," he had every day in prison. The clock radio clicked on and the voice of Smiley O'Reilly on the clock radio fully wakes him to his new reality. He was free now, at Gord and Irma's, and good ol' Smiley O'Reilly was still the morning man at CNJK. Man, that guy had to be about 70 now.

After he showers, shaves and dresses, Mouse goes into the kitchen, where Irma has left breakfast, a slice of her famous strudel on a plate covered with saran wrap, a glass of orange juice with a paper crown, and another paper crown, upside down, with a big pink vitamin pill on it, next to a note.

"Good Morning. Gord and Lisa have gone to get their Dad and I've gone to work. The numbers are on the fridge under the Macosham Motors magnet. How about strudel for breakfast? Heat this plate in the microwave on high for 2 minutes. There's coffee too, ready to go. Just push the big blue button."

Mouse looks up and sees a yellow post-it stuck to a coffee machine with an empty cup under its spout.

"Please turn off the coffeemaker after you're done. If you want to go out, the bus schedule is on the fridge under the magnet. Bus E47 stops at the NW corner by the newspaper box. It will take you to the new Eastgate Mall. Fare is $4, exact change. There are coins in the jar on top of the fridge if you need them. I'll be home around 2, half day at work today. Don't answer the phone for strangers. Love ya, Irma."

Strudel for breakfast. Irma had underlined the word, so she wanted him to take notice. Message received, he thought. How many people get strudel for breakfast, and this strudel, Irma's strudel, so flaky and buttery, the filling tart and spicy?

Experience! Savor! Appreciate! As Dr. Lobo would say. Mouse does, eating slowly to prolong the pleasure, appreciating this good thing and Irma for making it.

As he eats, he studies the bus schedule, then looks at the newspaper, which is open at the financial section where oil prices are listed. First thing Irma checks every day, the commodities, as this economy and everyone they know depends on their rise and fall. He flips to the funnies, then to the sports pages, when the phone rings. The LED screen on the phones says "SECRET GINGER," so he answers.

"Hi Ginger," he says.

"It's Leo. Mom's driving. Who's this?"

"Mouse."

"Mouse?"

In the background, Ginger says, "Mouse? Put it on speaker, Leo. Thanks. Mouse! You're home! How the hell are you, you son of a bee?"

"I'm good, eh. You?"

"Yeah, we're good. Tell Irma and Gord we'll be there for Christmas Eve. And if the cops call or Randy calls, you haven't spoken to me."

"Okay."

"Good to have you back, Mouse." She clicks off.

About five minutes later the phone rings again, from a number in area code 587. He doesn't know where that is, so he doesn't answer. After he finishes his breakfast, he washes his plate and silverware, putting them in the white Rubbermaid dish rack, gets four dollars in coins from the jar on top of the fridge, then reconsiders and takes four more so he'll have enough change to get home.

An icy wind blows down from the Arctic. His coat is not enough for the wind, and he goes back inside to find a warmer one. The only spare coat that looks like it will fit him is a dusty brown suede coat, a straight cut hunter's coat with a fur collar and heavy plaid quilting inside. It hangs on a hook above a pair of rubber boots. The coat fits nicely, but the boots are way too big, so he has to wear his white prison shoes, and gloves of course, to keep his hands warm, with some toilet paper stuffed into one socket to hide the missing tip of one finger.

The first thing he does when he leaves is take the cigar out of the lawn Santa's mouth and put it in the concrete urn by the porch, as Gord instructed.

It's a strange sensation to be out on the street, walking free. The houses look pretty much the same but the cars are different. He knows what the new models look like from television. Still, it's strange to see them now on a familiar street. To distract himself from the peculiar feeling, he studies the cars as he walks to the bus stop. Has to know about the new cars if he hopes to work in his Uncle Murph's junkyard. As he peers in the window of a new Chevy to study the dashboard, a neighbor walking across the streets stops and watches, frowning.

"Nice car," Mouse says, and waves, then awkwardly walks away, feeling the neighbor's eyes at every step.

When the bus comes, he asks the driver to let him know when they get to the new Eastgate mall.

"It's end of the line," the driver says. "The Voice will tell you."

The Voice? The doors close and a woman's automated voice says, "Next stop Sylvan Park."

Mouse laughs. The motherfucking bus is talking to him! The few other passengers look at him, puzzled. He sits by a window to look at the town, almost the same but not quite. The Crown Burger is gone, replaced by a McDonald's, but Sweet Cream Bakery and the Hungarian butcher are still there. Candy's Cafe is no more and same for the Red River Diner. Now it's Tim Horton's and Starbuck's. The cars are newer, the pedestrians all talking on cell phones.

The Voice says, "Next stop South Street Manor," and Mouse thinks, this is what a time traveller would feel like, or Rip Van Winkle.

Then: "Next stop Eastgate Mall Station."

A woman greeter inside the main doors of the new mall hands him a map.

"Thank you," he says. "I need shoes."

She looks down at his shoes, and then back up at him. She has just checked him out and he comes up wanting, but he imagines she recognizes the shoes, bright white Ked-like shoes, scotch-guarded to resist stains, standard issue at Elk Woods. In the winter, they were made invisible in the white snowy yard of the prison, and from a distance it looked like the inmates had no feet, like they floated, or hovered, two inches above the ground.

"Foot Locker, K4, on the second level," the greeter says.

When he walks away, his feet feel heavier and the shoes seem to glow radioactive. He will get new shoes, black ones that don't announce his shameful past. What woman would love him now, an ex-con and a former crackhead? What a catch.

But first he has to find his way to K4. He walks half the length of the ground floor, past every sort of thing someone can buy, clothes, flowers, books, electronics, cosmetics, chocolates, toys, bath bombs and soap, motorcycle gear, things made out of twigs and stones, 40 flavors of popcorn from a popcorn cart, keychains with insects encased in plexiglass, t-shirts and mugs for the World's Best Grandmas.

At the center of the mall he takes an escalator up to the second floor, and finds Foot Locker with relative ease. Does the clerk who fits him for the new shoes recognize the white ones? He's not sure. Then it doesn't matter. He wears the black shoes out, and drops the shameful white ones into the nearest trash receptacle.

He has some gifts he made at Elk Woods and brought with him to Gord and Irma's, but he feels he needs to get more, nice store bought things for everyone to make some amends. Show them how much he cares. Even people who only show up for Christmas Eve are on the list, like Goofy, aka Joey Minot, a good friend of Mouse's from their foster care days. Say his name three times and he appears, like Beetlejuice, to sit on the couch silently, nursing one beer all night, not talking. Offer him a choice of two or more things, and Goofy would be paralyzed by indecision, so Irma always just made a plate with some of everything for him and he dutifully ate it all.

Well, Mouse empathizes with him, because he feels lost in this humongous mall with too many choices. He checks out a few stores, is overwhelmed by the profusion of things, and heads for the Food Court to take a break.

So many kinds of fast food, not just burgers, donairs, and pizza, but two Japanese counters, a Korean Barbecue, a Chinese buffet, a Ukrainian pierogi stand, the Mongolian Grill, Happy Mushroom Vegetarian, and something called Addis Ababa Ethiopian Food. What was that, he wondered? Should he try it? Ah, KFC. Yes. He'd craved it in prison and tried to recreate it in the prison kitchen, but there's nothing like the real thing. Four piece extra crispy with slaw, fries and gravy, and a coke, and a takeaway order to bring back to Irma and Gord's.

He has never eaten anything more delicious.

The food court seating area fills up for lunch, mostly younger people who stare and tap into smart phones as they eat.

But across the food court, a woman his age fixes him with a curious look that says the same thing he's thinking about her, "Who are you, you look familiar?" He recognizes her first. Lindy Cowell. Hasn't seen her since junior high school. He blushes. She smiles slightly, then she recognizes him and her face contorts into some kind of rictus of distaste so strong that she picks up her tray, and moves to another table, her back to him.

Mouse feels that sick feeling again. He takes out a notebook, and as Dr. Lobo instructed, names his feelings: Fear, Shame, Embarrassment, Loneliness, Longing, Regret.

Then he writes down: You can't change the Past. Justify a better Present and Future by living a better life NOW.

Showing gratitude is living a better life. Okay, so, presents. Irma likes books, mysteries and romances mainly. But which of these many, many books has she not read already? He has no clue. He stares at rows of possibilities, stunned like Goofy, until a helpful young clerk man asks, "Can I help you?"

Mouse explains his problem.

"What you need is a gift certificate, then they can choose their own books."

What a brilliant idea. One for Irma, and one for Lisa, who likes books too but her tastes change every few years. Gord and Norm get Canadian Tire Gift certificates. But gift certificates in envelopes look so unimpressive, he feels a need to add something of substance, something in a box. Ah. Purdy's chocolates, in purple and gold boxes. Classy. Ten boxes please.

At a hobby shop he buys a few things for Goofy and Gord. Then, at a shop called Lush, a friendly young greeter waves him in, and he can't resist her bright smile and the heady perfume of the shop. It's a veritable Aladdin's Cave of colorful, jewel-like soaps and jellies and bath fizzies, where the staff fuss over him, and he leaves with two bags of stuff, and four dollars exact change for the bus home.

On the way out, the young greeter says, "You're going to make some people very merry this Christmas."

Just like that, he feels happy. She didn't have to say that. He'd already spent his money in her store. But she said it anyway, with that big bright smile, and this is all it takes now to make his day.

# 6

# BRAD FITS THE BILL

Tammy chooses her rides carefully, and has since she was a girl. Years ago, she had a friend, Cindy Crowchild, a native girl she was in foster care with, until they ran away at age 14 to work on a pot harvest. Cindy took a ride with another guy on the harvest to get back to her granny on a reservation not served by any public transit for miles. The guy seemed very nice, good looking too. All the women on the crew had a little crush on him. After the harvest he was to deliver some of the product to Fort MacMurray, then drop Cindy at the reservation on his way down to Edmonton to deliver the rest. She never got home and the marijuana was never delivered. A hunter found her remains a year later, in the bush.

Tammy tried to burn that man's face into her brain, in case she saw it again. Of course he'd be older now, more than twenty years older, and probably changed the way he looked, fatter, with a moustache and beard maybe. By now, there were so many of those faces burned into her brain the old ones had grown fainter and she sometimes confused people with other people because of the drugs. Nevertheless, she nursed a fantasy of running into one of these men again, whipping out one of the sharp knives concealed on her body, and stabbing him in the heart.

So she doesn't end up like Cindy Crowchild, she tries to pick men at truck stops where they seem well known, men who seem kind, older, and smaller in size so she has a decent chance of fighting them if things go bad. If there's a woman driver, she'll first try to cadge a ride with her, but it's usually men on these routes. She strikes up a conversation, and makes sure she asks for a ride when the waitress or bartender is near, makes sure the waitress hears.

She doesn't see a safe-looking man in the truck stop coffee shop when she's let off there by the previous ride she hitched, so she sits at the bar and talks and jokes to the bartender, a young woman, as she sips a coffee, making sure the woman takes note of her. After about fifteen minutes, three drivers come in, and one of them, Brad, fits the bill and agrees to drive her to Nojack.

When he chats her up in the truck cab, Tammy tells him her name is Danielle, and she's trying to get home to see her family for Christmas after visiting an uncle in a mining camp, but she lost her wallet and phone, or maybe it was stolen—she can't be sure when or where it happened. A total lie but it's always good to make them think there are people expecting you who can and will do something if you don't show up.

Her father, she says, is vice-president of the Brewers' Transport Union, a real thing and a real guy who is not her father but met her once when she was working in a bar. Wouldn't know her from Adam now, but he's someone with standing who could get action and what harm is there in using his name if he'll never find out? Everyone knows you don't mess with the beer truck drivers. Tammy can't get away with anything too high-falutin, like posing as a rich, classy woman like Patricia Winter. This is much more plausible. The important thing is

38

to make the man know there is someone who cares about you, who will miss you, who will be taken seriously, and be able to do something about it.

The driver talks a bit about his family Christmas, how they have a goose because his wife's grandmother was English, so it became a family tradition and they always have a goose at Christmas and a plum pudding steeped in brandy with a sweet treacle sauce, and they have their turkey and pumpkin pie on Boxing Day.

"Then we have the airing of grievances and feats of strength," he says.

"What?" She says.

"You know, Festivus. From Seinfeld?"

"Oh, I only saw one episode. It wasn't for me." Whiskey watched that show, when she was with him, but Tammy thought it was ridiculous. Who cared about someone who was a close-talker when there were bigger things to worry about? Who were those people with their petty shitty little problems?

Tammy describes her family Christmas—not the real ones, charity baskets in musty basement suites with grey carpet stained by flooding—but Irma's Christmases, large and noisy with lots of food and beer and music, as she remembers from when she was with Mouse and before that, Whiskey.

"And karaoke," she says. "That's my favorite part, and Mouse's too—"

"Mouse?"

"My husband. He does Rammstein at karaoke, and you'd think it was Rammstein."

"Mouse, eh? Little guy?"

"No, not at all, it's like, an opposite nickname." A total lie, but let this guy believe she has a big brute waiting for her at home.

"Oh right. I guess they'd call me Big Guy then, or Curly. Heh. You want some coffee?"

He nods to a thermos in the holder between them.

Tammy pulls a bottle of Coca-Cola from her pocket.

"No thanks, I'm set. Want me to pour you a coffee?" She says.

"Uh, no, that's fine. I got caffed up at the diner."

Wants her to drink something he isn't drinking? Yeah, like she'd fall for that. And did she imagine it, or did he seem disappointed she wouldn't drink his coffee, just a trace of letdown in the eyes, the corners of the mouth?

"Thanks anyway," she says. She makes as if looking out the window but watching his reflection in it out of the corner of her eye, another trick she picked up along the way. When she turns back to him she catches her own reflection in the side mirror. It's always jarring, to see her face, so much older than the face she still sees in her mind. She's not a young pretty girl any more. Will Mouse even recognize her, when she barely can?

"What does Mouse do?" Brad asks.

"He drives a beer truck."

"This is his busy time of year."

"Yeah, this and summer."

"And Stanley Cup and Grey Cup."

Mouse might be her last chance, she thinks, and for all his many faults, he truly loved her and believed in her dreams. Mouse would never leave her, or beat her, or even call her bad names. Mouse went to prison for her.

If she could just get him away from those horrible friends of his.

# 7

# TOUCH THE LUCKY DOLLAR

"Tammy called last night," Gord says, as he pulls the car onto the range road.

"What?"

"Hold on 'til I clear this," He switches lanes to get out from behind a logging truck and guns the gas to get past the truck before any oncoming traffic appears, since it's just a two lane highway at this point and accidents are frequent. The logging trucks drive slowly and they are long, so there's always a risk of getting caught in the middle when some yahoo is speeding in the opposite direction. Still, the alternative, sitting behind one for miles, is worse.

Once Gord's past the truck, he picks up the thread. "She got some guy to call, claiming he was a friend of Mouse's dad—"

"Mouse's dad had no friends," Lisa says.

"This guy put Tammy on the line. Irma threatened to beat the crap outta her if she even sets foot in Alberta."

"Did you tell Mousie?"

"We haven't even told him she ran off with Darryl yet. Guess she's left Darryl, or he left her."

"Hey!" Lisa catches the reflection of a cop car in the rear view mirror. She turns around. Yes, it is Officer Diane DiMara and her embarrassed partner Officer Oleanik, looking down at his lap, his eyes shielded with his hand.

DiMara is following too closely, until the county line. Beyond that she cannot go. Lisa watches the cop car's reflection shrink in the rear view mirror.

"She's still harassing you?" Gord says.

"Dumber than a sack of hammers too. She thinks I know where my ex is? She's the cop. Let her find him."

"She's nuts. How did she become a cop?"

"Legacy cop because of her dad." Say no more. They laugh at some shared memory about the late Officer Bob DiMara who was as much of a dumbass as his daughter.

"That's a long grudge she has against you Lisa, since high school."

"Long grudges? Look at Whiskey and Mouse! LOOK AT MURPH AND MOUSE'S DAD!"

"Look at Murph and our dad and their long feud over that failed beekeeping venture."

"It wasn't a complete disaster," Lisa says.

A private joke. Hysterical laughter. Hysterical stories. The "fishing" trips, The table-turning bar brawls, the Get Rich schemes like chinchillas, Fuller Brush, and cellar mushrooms, the Big Argument, the fighting.

"Jesus," Lisa gasps through sobs of laughter, "The revenge."

"They were both so good at revenge." Gord stops laughing and a nanosecond later, Lisa does too.

"Fuck."

"Fuck."

"We've invited Murph so we can all suck up to him and maybe he'll give Mousie a job, and Dad will be there too Christmas Eve."

"Should we turn around? Not get Dad?" Gord asks. "He doesn't want to come anyway. He'll be happier having Christmas Dinner at the Hinton Hotel. We can bring him in for the new year instead."

"He has to come. He has a doctor's appointment on the 27th and he's already missed two appointments."

"I'll figure out something, a system to keep Dad and Murph apart."

"Thanks, Gord. I'd hate to see Mousie's first Christmas home in seven years wrecked by those two. What are we going to do about Whiskey? You know he'll come by on Christmas Eve at some point."

"Yeah, I figured Mouse and I could leave and do a beer run. Whiskey knows about the lawn Santa and the stogie. I told him."

Before Edson, they stop at a favorite diner, the Lucky Dollar Bar & Grill, so named because the original owner had glued silver dollars to the walls, back when people paid with them like regular currency.

They breathe in the crisp mountain air, just a hint of the pulp mill, not enough to overpower the smell of pine trees, cold ozone, and truck exhaust as they walk into the Dollar. Inside the door they touch the first silver dollar, the Lucky one, glued to the archway inside, for good luck, and take stools at the bar, since all the tables are taken by Yuppie skiers drinking Bloody Marys and lattes, and grungy old miners and lumbermen drinking Red Eyes—beer and tomato juice—and black coffee.

43

"Nice to see the Lucky Dollar is still here among all the strip malls and fast food joints," Lisa says to the bartender, a young woman with a ruby red stud in her nose.

"The new owner is thinking of doing a wall in shiny golden Loonies, and changing the name to the Lucky Loonie," the bartender tells them before taking their order for coffee and the House Special Breakfast Sandwich #1 (apple cheese muffin, split in the middle, toasted panini style, buttered, and stuffed with crispy bacon and a dollop of maple mustard), and House Special Breakfast Sandwich #2 (a maple glazed raised donut, toasted, split in the middle and filled with a scrambled egg patty, back bacon, and a dollop of maple mustard), both sandwiches cut in half so they could share.

"Who bought it?"

"TKG Enterprises, a hospitality company. They plan to franchise the Lucky Dollar, maybe take it nationwide," the bartender says, before she goes to get their coffee and muffins.

"Well, even the Lucky Dollar has sold out," Gord says. "Can't blame people for selling, I mean put your life into something and then it's time to retire, you should get rich. But man, I dunno."

"The corporatization of everything," Lisa says. "I hope they don't change the name of this place at least. I don't care what they call the franchises."

"Why does it matter?"

"I dunno, but it does."

All the phones in the cafe suddenly ring with an alarm, most at the same moment, a few staggering afterwards. It's an Amber Alert, about Ginger and Leo, which resounds throughout the cafe.

"Fuck"

"Fuck."

Gord calls to the bartender. "Can you make that order to go?" The bartender pours their coffee into takeout cups and snaps open a brown paper bag.

They touch the Lucky dollar again on the way out, this time with meaning.

"We pick up dad, then we circle back, find out where Ginger is, and intercept her, and then we'll bring them home." Gord says, starting the car and pulling out. He sees Lisa's look. "She's doing the right thing, Lisa. It's Christmas."

"She's doing the right thing but it's also illegal. She could lose all visitation rights." Lisa sees Gord's look. "Maybe that's why DiMara was tailing us. They probably think we know where Ginger is, and we'd probably do more harm than good trying to head her off."

"You're right."

"Let's focus on Dad, that's enough dysfunction for one day."

Gord relaxes. Lisa turns on the radio and finds a station of Christmas carols.

"Wait," Gord says. "Driving a grey BMW?"

"Eh?"

"The Amber Alert says she's driving a grey BMW. Where the hell would Ginger get a grey BMW? She drives a blue Toyota."

"Murph. I'll bet you a toonie. She got the logos and fake plates from Murph's junkyard."

Gord smiles. "Ginger may pull this off."

"Yeah? Where's the first place the cops are going to look on Christmas Eve? Your house. Randy will know she'll want to bring Leo to the party. He'll tell the cops. We'll all be accessories. Boy would Officer Miz DiMara love that."

"When we get to Hinton, I'll call Irma, and she can call Eddie Redfeather. He still has some pull." He laughs ruefully. "Took your mind off Dad for a bit anyway."

"Dad." One word that contains universes of meaning for them. Lisa turns the radio back up and lights a cig. "Jesus."

"What else is going to come up? Merry Fucking Christmas."

Neither notices the semi passing them in the opposite direction. They couldn't have been able to see past the driver anyway, to the passenger who hitched a ride. Tammy.

The sun moves from behind a mountain and hits them in the eyes. They put on their shades. The light glints off the grey in Gord's hair, more grey every year, and he's hunched more over the steering wheel, bad back and two trick knees, 62 and still doing pipeline work, when oil prices were high. When they were low, everyone was strained, especially now that Glassco was automating more and had already outsourced most of the manufacturing.

The future was going to smack them all in the face, Lisa feared, and not a damned thing any of them could do about it.

They were, after all, the children of an old dinosaur like their father, "Slim" as he was known, who had gone back to the bush to live off the land once their mother divorced him. He swore he wouldn't return to civilization until she was dead, but after she died he made no move to return. He liked his life, or perhaps, hated it less than any other life he might have been living. If Dad's family had a crest it would show two bulls butting heads, Lisa thinks, and the motto would be, "Living in the past, denying the present, and hiding from the future."

46

Gord reads her mind. "I've been thinking about Mouse, and what things he missed while he was away and will have to adjust to, and it made me think about Dad too. You know? The time warp of it all."

"Yeah, I get it. Dad lives out there like it's 1934, and there's always something that discombobulates him about the 'future' as he refers to the present and recent past. He wasn't always like that. Well, he was a little, about women, and LGBT—"

"A little? Don't start. But he was modern in some ways. He liked technology back then. Now he lives like Fred Flintstone and we must look to him like the Jetsons."

"Bingo."

Hinton is close enough now that they can smell the pulp mill, the odd smell somewhere between bread yeast and urine. It summons up a series of memory flashes for Lisa, of previous trips to visit Dad, like the last reunion up on Dad's trapline, when he got drunk, got his rifle, accused Gord, his spitting image, of really being the kid of some long-ago neighbour named McKay with a glass eye who was "always sweet on Gladys," their mother. Gord, the gentle giant, who'd do anything for their father, with saintly Christian patience and love. It was Lisa who took their dad to task, and sometimes his daughter-in-law Irma, but it was Gord he'd always gone after, Gord he hurt most.

"I hope Dad is on good behavior," she says.

"He's softer now that he's old and sick."

"More sandpaper, less gravel?"

"Might well be our last Christmas with him."

"I know."

# 8

# ANDY WHY

When Ginger and Leo pull in, Andy Why is sitting on his porch in a rocking chair with a shotgun in his lap. The grow op has been a legal op for two years, and he has never once fired the gun, but right now it makes him feel better, knowing it looks intimidating to anyone who might be following Ginger. Even more effective are the five llamas that "guard" him. The llamas are not intimidating, per se, but they add a confusion factor to set miscreants off balance.

Ginger rolls in fast leaving a backwash of spitting gravel in her wake, then stops suddenly right in front of the porch. Andy comes down, opens the passenger side and grabs Leo.

"Put the car in the back garage," Andy says, referring to the second secret garage he used when this was an illegal op, back in the bush and underground. "Then get inside. I'll fix you some food while we wait for the doctor. I got a call in to a lawyer too but got his voicemail. Everyone's gone for the holidays."

Leo follows Uncle Andy into the big old farmhouse, grinning and chattering about the llamas, Sid, Harvey, Lucy, Bob and, of course, Dalai, while Ginger drives around back.

When she gets into the house, Leo is halfway through a sandwich.

"Want a PB&J?" Andy asks. "My own J—saskatoon and blueberry."

"Yeah. Thanks. You changed the place. I like the vintage fridge," she says. "Like the one we grew up with, the old Frigidaire in that dull aqua colour."

"Yeah. It's original body but all new works. I've been collecting mid century stuff, like Gord and Irma. Milk or coffee?"

"Coffee. Where can I? You know."

"Back porch, sun room."

In the grip of a massive nic fit, Ginger half runs to the back porch.

"You want more milk, Leo?"

He nods as he pops the last corner of sandwich into his mouth.

"And another PB&J?"

Leo nods again and swallows.

"So what were you saying, before your mom so ruuuuudely interrupted us."

Leo smiles. "Dad and Mother make me do this weird stuff at church."

"Linda makes you call her Mother? Do not tell your mother that. Call Randy's wife, Linda."

"Okay. So anyway—I have to stand for this part."

"Please."

"There's always a big sermon and—"

"Holy crap, Leo, you've grown a few inches."

"Yeah. The pastor talks about sin, and something in the news, and shame, and how Jesus suffered to wash away our sins with his blood, then he says things and we say them, with our arms in the air, and shaking, like this."

Leo puts his arms straight up, and begins to shake all over.

"I'm a dirty sinner. Bathe me in the blood of Jesus. We line up and the pastor touches our heads and screams that we are bathed in the blood of Jesus, and we yell, Hallelujah!"

"Jeez. That's nuts, but at least you see that. Don't ever forget that. Those people are the opposite of Jesus, the opposite, and what's the opposite of Jesus?"

✻✻✻

The sunroom has rockers like Grandma Lupinski's. Reproductions, it looks like, but the same classic build, with embroidered cushions on the seats and backs. Andy has a rocking habit which probably came from being somewhere on that autism spectrum. It was one of the things that bonded him and Grandma Lupinski, his foster mother for many years. She noticed he liked to rock and got him a rocking chair. They'd sit on the porch and rock together, inspiring the expected jokes and nicknames, "Rockin' Grandma," "Rockin' out," etc. Grandma Lupinski taught him how to darn socks and they became "The Rockin' Sockin' Twosome." She also taught him how to put up preserves and use a table saw.

Thinking of Grandma Lupinski makes Ginger mist up. Grandma Lupinski always seemed to know just what a kid needed to feel happy and useful and loved. Boy, that was rare. For a moment, she feels like Grandma Lupinski is sitting in the chair next to her. It's a powerful visceral feeling that comes like a sudden warm wind. There's comfort in it, even now, 15 years since grandma passed on.

The sliding screen door opens and Andy comes out with the sandwich and the coffee.

"Thanks, Andy."

"Leo had a growth spurt, eh?"

"Oh I know. That hurt, seeing him so changed, having missed out on four Inches of his life."

Andy notes a different kind of growth spurt in Ginger, in the opposite direction. While she probably isn't shorter, her posture's bad, and the slight stoop makes her appear shorter. Her blonde hair is going silver in places, and she has more lines around her eyes, all pointing slightly downward since losing custody to Randy.

"So I've got a doctor coming, he used to buy marijuana from me for his cancer patients before it was legal, known him forever. He's cool. But we are not going to tell him any details or your real names," Andy says. "If he doesn't know, he's not an accomplice. He'll examine Leo, write a report we can give a lawyer if I can get one on the horn today and we'll try to see a judge—"

"Okay."

"It's not going to be easy, Ginger. You abducted your kid."

"Because it's Christmas, and Christmas is everything to a kid."

"I know, I know. I agreed to help because we're kin, sort of, we're family, he's a kid, and it's fucking Christmas. You're doing the right thing but also the wrong thing, ya know? The right thing the wrong way."

Andy Why knows a bit about the "wrong" way from his youth, when his friends often found themselves asking him, "Andy, Why?" about various choices he had made from girlfriends to jobs. In retrospect though, Ginger has to admit now that some of those were good choices, for Andy, like buying the marijuana grow op, lock stock and barrel, including the llamas.

"If we could see a judge—"

"It's December 23rd and we don't have the bucks to grease the wheels. What's more, there's no guarantee a judge is going to see things your way, Ginger. You work in a stripper bar—"

"As a bartender. And there's nothing wrong with being a stripper anyway. It's her body she can do with it what she wants, eh? Your last girlfriend—"

"Not everyone is so liberal. You have a record."

"Shoplifting, it's years old, and the pot busts were expunged."

"And you are single with a history of shitty men, one of whom has reformed and is an upstanding Christian citizen now whose wife has a spotless reputation—"

"Upstanding?!"

"I'm putting this the way his lawyer will. I'm gonna help, but you're going to have to pay the piper for this after Christmas, even if you get away with it. Now, I've got a vehicle Goofy left here, his late grandpa's truck, you can drive that to Edmonton. Has Saskatchewan plates. I'll give you a burner phone that connects to a service in North Africa—"

"I have a burner phone."

"Good. I'll also give you a map of back roads and logging roads I used to take when I was illegal and drove pot into Alberta. I'll drive into Nojack separately. Does Randy know I'm here?"

"I don't think so. I didn't tell him."

"Good. So what else is new?"

"Mouse is out. He's living at Gord and Irma's. Hey, are you still in touch with Darryl?"

"No. Last I heard he and Tammy were in Vancouver somewhere, then they had a falling out and she was living with some dealer in St. Rupe."

Andy gets a text. "Doctor's here."

There is no strep, the doctor will certify, in "Child X" who is verified with Leo's inky fingerprint on the document. The lawyer does not call back.

# 9

# GOOFY'S AN ARTIST?

Irma comes home, and as soon as she opens the back door, a chill whistles through her heart. The peg, where her late father's coat usually hangs, is empty. His boots are still there, below, but his coat is gone.

Reason returns when she sees Mouse's coat hanging nearby. Of course he borrowed a warmer coat to go out and she doesn't mind. It makes her feel better knowing Mouse is wrapped up in her dad's coat. Her father was in that coat when he died. It was the last thing he touched while alive, his arms were in those sleeves, his feet in those boots, and they are the last physical connection to him, besides her DNA.

Mouse isn't back yet. After she puts down the groceries, she sees a message Mouse left that "Secret G" had called. Ginger had a burner phone of some kind, used prepaid credit cards to charge it up online, and Irma hadn't understood why until she read the second line of the message: "She has L. and they are on their way. Don't say anything to anyone. Destroy this message."

Irma burns the message in an ashtray. Yeah, she understands what Ginger is doing. But the price she might pay! Irma wants another cigarette, badly, but Gord has taken the tin with him to his dad's.

Being alone, she'd normally put on her dead dad's coat now, but Mouse is wearing it, and she never wears it around other people.

The back doorbell rings, and she hears the inner door open.

"Irma!" It's Whiskey.

He comes bounding in, doesn't wait for an invitation.

"That sonvabitch Mouse here?"

"No, he went Christmas shopping. What does the lawn Santa say?"

"Did you tell my kid he had to graduate high school?"

"What?"

"You saw him at the Safeway at lunch, you told him to get back into school?"

"Yeah, so what, Whiskey? You don't want your kid to get an education?"

"I only got ninth grade and I did fine. I still got 65,000 bucks in the bank."

"You won the lottery, Whiskey. These are different times than when we were kids. It's all tech and automation and robots. You want your kid up and down with oil prices, getting all sorts of injuries that will put him in a wheelchair like your old man?"

"And you told him he's invited for Christmas Eve but I'm not because Mouse will be here?"

"If you're not willing to forgive him and move on, then yes, you are not invited."

"He's the criminal, not me."

"Only because you weren't convicted, Whiskey. It's been years since Tammy went off with Mouse. Maybe you dodged a bullet. Maybe you would have gone to Elk Woods instead of Mouse. And don't give me that stuff about how Mouse ruined Tammy. You know damned well it's the other way around."

Whiskey can't meet Irma's glance. He storms out.

"Fuck you and fuck Christmas," Whiskey says.

"Put the stogey in the lawn Santa's mouth," Irma calls after him.

And he's gone.

Fifteen minutes later, the doorbell rings again. It's Officer Diane DiMara and her embarrassed partner Officer Oleanik.

"Irma, can we speak with you?" DiMara says. DiMara is really into the cop thing, has the swagger down. Keeps one hand on the gun at her waist while she speaks, as if she might need it speaking to Irma.

"Yeah, what is it?"

"You seen or heard from Ginger?"

"I haven't spoken to her in a couple of days. Why?"

"You didn't get the amber alert? Really?"

"What is this about?"

"Ginger has allegedly abducted her child Leo from his lawful custodians."

"Come on. Randy."

"He has a court order to keep Leo with him for the holidays because Leo has strep throat."

"Bet that's bullshit but in any event, I haven't spoken to her in days." This was not a lie. She hadn't actually spoken to her, and DiMara hadn't asked if she'd called and left a message with Mouse.

"I have a tip for you," Irma says. "Tammy is heading back to Alberta. Bet it's because they have a rap sheet on her in BC."

Officer DiMara hates Tammy even more than she hates Lisa, although nobody knows why. She nods earnestly at Irma.

"Thank you," she says. "Oh, uh, is that Mouse sitting outside on the curb?"

"What?"

Irma goes to the front window, and there's Mouse, wearing her father's jacket, sitting on the curb with a lot of shopping bags, half hidden by a car. She opens the front door and calls out, just as the cops leave, "Mouse, haul your ass in here."

Mouse hauls it, the bags flapping at his sides. The cops make him nervous.

"What were you doing out there?"

"There was no stogey in the lawn Santa's mouth. I thought Whiskey was here."

"That asshole didn't put the stogey back in. Let me take your coat—"

"Can I keep it on for a bit, Irma? I'm freezing."

"Sure."

"I forgot to buy tape. Do you have some, so's I can wrap all my presents?"

There are bags and bags in different colors from different shops, and the heady smell of Lush in the air.

"Yeah, the hall closet next to our room, second shelf. There's extra paper and ribbon too. Can I see what you got for everyone?"

"Well, no. I can show you the things I made at Elk Woods, or some of them."

Mouse goes into his room, comes out with what looks like a box wrapped in a sweater. It is a wooden box, about two feet long, a foot wide and three inches high.

"I made this for Goofy. It's an art box, eh, to put his paints and glue in."

"An art box?"

"For his paints and other stuff."

"Goofy paints?"

"Yeah. You didn't know that?"

"How would I, Mouse? If Goofy has said 25 words to me in the last twenty years—"

"Yeah, he makes a lot of stuff. I bought some paints and brushes for it at the mall. He probably has his own but this way, he knows what the box is for."

"How do you know this?"

"Goofy and I were good friends back in school. Cuz we was both left back two years in a row, eh? And he's smart!"

"Oh right. Did Goofy talk to you?"

"A little. Not much. He's shy, eh?"

"I know. Well, that's good you guys get along, because Goofy works for your uncle Murph and he finds Goofy kind of frustrating.  Of course, Murph is a handful himself."

Mouse decides he's warm enough and takes off the coat.

"I'm a bit chilly now," Irma says." Hand me the coat."

She puts it on. "Want some coffee? Gord and Lisa are bringing their Dad in from the bush and I don't know if they'll be home for dinner. I could make something or we could order in some Chinese and watch a Christmas movie."

"Oh, I brought us home some KFC," Mouse says.

"My hero!"

# 10

# STRAPPING YOUNG MINER

When Gord and Lisa pull up beside the Little Berland river, their dad Slim is not in his shack and it's the wrong time of the day, almost lunchtime, for him to be checking his trap lines. As a rule, he checked in the morning and before sunset, and they had carefully timed their trip to avoid these times, not just to make him easier to find but because neither approved of trapping, although he used the "humane" traps, and one thing you could say about old Slim was that he never took more from the land than he needed to survive and his miserly simple ways made him far greener than most people. The pelts he sold, according to wildlife quotas, and the meat he ate in a stew for him and whatever dogs he had at the time. Through the frosted window of his shack, Lisa can see the solar lamps he reads by and the solar powered radio that keeps him company, gifts from Lisa which replaced the old battery operated versions. The stove burns wood or coal but it didn't take much to heat up this small shack, well-insulated thanks to Gord. At night, Slim put some of the embers into an old fashioned bed warmer, and crawled into the sack with a warmed bed, a big down comforter, and whatever dogs he had at the time, to keep them all warm.

At the moment, he has no dogs. He told Irma he wanted one for Christmas, a full breed husky, and she promised him they would get him one in the new year. The plan though, is keep him with them in Nojack through a series of pleas, inducements, and deceptions, and not let him return to the bush.

"Where do you think he is, Hinton or Grande Cache," Lisa asks.

"You call the bar at the Hinton hotel and I'll call Dolly in Grande Cache. If he went into town he would have hit a bar."

He wasn't in Hinton, but Dolly, who owns and operates the Grande Cache Inn, knows where he is.

"Slim's in jail here in GC," Dolly says on speaker. "Him and the guy he punched in the face in the tavern last night. Do you have any cash on you? ATM is out of order here."

"Some," Gord says. "Not sure it's enough for bail."

"Not just bail, Gord, but the guy he hit is gonna want something. You can haggle him down by shaming him," Dolly says. "He was provoking your dad all night, and then your dad decked him. He's a big strapping young miner, and he got decked by a man more than fifty years his senior."

"Come on, Dolly. If Dad decked him it's because Dad sucker punched him, below the belt probably," Lisa says. She takes Dolly's silence for confirmation.

"I don't want to blackmail the guy," Gord says.

"Look it's gonna be a third strike for your old man, and frankly, he is getting too old to live on that trap line."

"Not too old to deck a strapping young miner."

"He's 83. The Mounties are pissed off at him and worried about the old buzzard, they're ready to send him to prison just to make sure he has steady medical care and three squares. I'd loan you the money for bail but I'm cash poor right now, renovations at the hotel and Christmas—"

"No worries, Dolly, we'll figure it out."

"Merry Fucking Christmas, Lisa."

"You too, Dolly."

There's a crash in the background, breaking glass.

"Shit. I have to go."

Dolly clicks off.

"Dad will have to tell us where the money is."

"He won't."

"He has to."

✶✶✶

"I haven't told you all this time, why should I tell you now?" Slim says. "That guy had it coming. You gotta smoke?"

"You can't smoke in jail, Dad. You can't smoke in prison either," Lisa says. "Which is where they want to send you unless we get you out of this jam. That takes money. Where is your money?"

Their dad looks at Lisa, looks at Gord, then looks back at Lisa.

"I'll tell you, but I won't tell him."

Lisa rolls her eyes. Gord sighs and says, "Okay, Dad. I'll leave you two alone."

When Gord is gone, Slim says, "There is no money."

"Well then, you have to stay in jail."

Slim is wearing the same damned flannel shirt and baggy oilcloth trousers he was wearing the last time they saw him, late October, and probably the same undershirt and undershirts too. He smells like rancid cheese and onions. If only he would face at least a few facts and give up the trap line. Just then, he looks so old and frail to her, his face as ridged and weathered as old bark, his moles sprouting white wiry hairs. If he didn't drop dead of a coronary while manning his traps, something else might get him, a grizzly, or one of those strapping young miners might come back to get revenge or rob him.

Now Lisa and Slim have a staring contest, but he with his rheumy wet old eyes is no match for her. He blinks.

"So? Lisa says.

"I ain't saying' nothing'"

"Okay then,"Lisa says, and gets up to go.

"Where are you going?"

"I'm dying for a smoke, and you want to spend Christmas in jail so then I am going back to Nojack—"

"Come here, Lisa." In a whisper Lisa can only just hear, Slim says, "It's buried in tobacco tins."

"Where?"

"Outside my shack, where my dog's graves are."

"You buried your money with your dead dogs?"

"No, I buried the dogs in secret spots, and put their grave markers above the tobacco tins to fool robbers. Take only what you need. I'll check later. Don't tell Gord. He'll steal it."

"You have a shovel out there?"

Slim throws her his keys. "In the shack."

"I'll be back Dad."

"Don't take too long. Havin' a nic fit here," he says.

After they bail him out, Lisa asks Slim if he needs to use the gents'. He insists he doesn't but it isn't long before he complains he needs to piss, so they stop at the Lucky Dollar for a bathroom break and fresh coffee. The place is bereft of yuppie skiers heading to Jasper now, just truckers and miners, men, so for once Lisa gets in and out of the women's room faster than the men, orders coffee and sandwiches to go, and runs into an old boyfriend, Denny.

"Denny, you're looking good," she says. "Glad to see you're out."

"You sound so surprised. Yeah, I'm out on parole, and dried out, working a job for Eddie Redfeather in Little Smoky, got a lady up there. I hear Mouse is out too."

Then he tells her something she wishes she hadn't heard, and can't tell anyone else, especially Irma. Irma would never get it out of her mind.

Denny grabs his coffee and goes when Slim comes out.

"Great to see ya agin, Lisa," Denny says and dashes..

Slim wants to stop for a beer before they make the last leg to Nojack. What the hell, he's not driving. Then he tries to leave with it, and the bartender stops him without stopping her conversation with some greasy guy from the oil patch. No doubt she's done this before.

"Dad, you can only drink that on-premises," Gord says.

Slim downs it in three swallows and pounds it on the counter when done.

"Thanks, sweetie," he says to the waitress, and plops down a five dollar tip.

"Merry Christmas, Slim."

"Yeah, merry fucking Christmas."

The beer means another pit stop before Nojack, Slim complaining about the government until Lisa turns up Christmas carols to drown it out. They haven't told him that Murph is coming to the Christmas Eve party, so's they can get a job for Mouse. Irma has volunteered to do that.

"Don't forget to stop at the Safeway," Lisa says. "I need to pick up some snack platters."

"We didn't need all the fancy food and crap for Christmas when I was a kid." Slim is off and running.

# 11

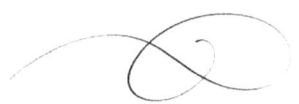

## TRUST IN GORD

"Goofy's an artist."

Irma still can't believe she missed this all these years.

"Yeah, he makes those presents he gives every year. Hand me the cranberries."

"I think we have enough garland, Mouse."

"Gotta have the popcorn and cranberry though, tradition."

"Goofy made The birdhouses?"

"Yeah."

"Damn. The garden sculptures?"

They hear the sound of Christmas carols approaching, loud but muted car music. Then they hear the car pull in.

"Gord and Lisa are home."

Mouse looks out the window.

"With Slim."

They exchange a look.

Irma answers it. "I'm gonna talk to Slim, and Gord is devising a system to keep Slim and Murph apart. He's got certain people involved to help out. It's not hard to distract Murph, right? So we just have to deal with Slim."

"Trust in Gord," Mouse says, and they both laugh. Gord, who never went on the gang's robberies back in the day, but would end up helping to plan them. Any problem that arose, Gord would find a solution or "devise a system."

"Trust in Gord."

On cue, Gord comes through the door, followed by Slim then Lisa.

"Gotta beer," Slim asks. "Been a helluva day."

"Merry Christmas, Slim," Irma says, giving him a hug before taking his coat.

"Yeah yeah."

"He's already had a beer," Lisa says.

Slim waves his hand in a light air slap and laughs. "See how my daughter looks out for my health, but it's okay, strong as an ox, gimme a beer, Irma."

If Gord had said it, Lisa thinks, Slim would have been belligerent and hurtful. She sighs.

"I'll get it for you Dad." They don't want him to get drunk, because then he'll go on about his late ex-wife Gladys and pick arguments with everyone. But no worries. Gord has devised a system. He and Lisa go to the garage and empty a Labatt's into a cup for Lisa, and replace it through a funnel with one of Andy's near beers. She grabs one for Andy too, and Molsons for Gord and Irma.

"Beer's a bit skunky," Slim complains, but drinks it as they eat. Irma keeps heaping food on his plate. Slim has a big appetite, always did but it's worse now thanks to his bad health, hyperthyroidism, anemia, and assorted minor pains. Strong as a sick, old ox, perhaps. Feeding him keeps him from talking. When the meal is done and he's starting to get sleepy, Irma lets Lisa give him a real Labatt's and she sets him up in his room while he drinks it.

"I got the goose down pillows you like, and the comforter," Irma says. "Don't smoke in here. Don't sleep in your clothes, or NAKED. Pajamas in the drawer and a bathrobe in the closet. WEAR THEM."

"Yeah yeah. I know."

"I like to remind you. Listen. Mouse needs a job, we're hoping to get him one at Murph's junkyard—"

"That son of a bitch? Mouse is better off being a hobo."

"No he's not. What a silly thing to say. Look Pop, it's Christmas, goodwill to men. Just ignore him, eh? If you don't, I'll tell Gord and Lisa everything I know."

They exchange a look. Irma means business.

"Yeah yeah," he says.

# DECEMBER 24, 2021

# 12

## ANDY WHY

At 3 a.m., Andy wakes Leo and brings him downstairs for breakfast, letting Ginger sleep in. He wants to talk to Leo alone.

"Eggs and bacon or eggs and tempeh?"

"Eggs and bacon."

"Brown toast only, but I made the bread myself."

"Thanks Uncle Andy."

"Your mom is an amazing mother, you know that, right? When your dad was messed up, she's the one who made sure you got what you needed."

"I know."

"I bet you appreciate her much more than you did before you moved in with Randy and Linda."

"I do!"

"Funny how that works. What do they say about Ginger?"

"It's weird, I mean, they call her a sinner, like, a really big sinner, but that it's their job as Christians to love her anyway. It's how you can tell you're a really good Christian, by how much you can love unlovable sinners, like, you hate the sin but —"

"Love the sinner."

"Yeah."

"That's bullshit, Leo. It's a form of narcissism, shaming, and control. You know what narcissism is?"

"Loving yourself."

"Loving yourself too much, sort of. It's more complicated. I've been watching the Pastor Wayne's videos. Those people, what they are really saying is, I am so healed and full of God's love, I can love almost anyone, maybe even you. It's condescending and mean. You understand?"

"Yeah."

"Jesus didn't die so you could be shamed and made to suffer. Opposite! He was all about the love and brotherhood, the wine and food, chilling out. He was not about judging, in fact, he said, judge not, lest ye be judged. I'm not saying you should be like Jesus. The dude was divine reportedly, we're mere mortals. Best we can do is our best."

"Okay."

"Remember this because those people are manipulative and they brainwash people. I'll get you a burner phone so you can call me if you need to."

Ginger is up. They can hear water running in the bathroom upstairs. When she wanders downstairs, Andy has her breakfast set up in the sunroom so she can stoke up on nicotine before they leave in Goofy's grandfather's pickup at 4 a.m. When they go, Andy gives them a big insulated cooler packed with food and drinks, two wigs, a small black

71

wig for Leo, a short black woman's wig for Ginger, and two pairs of fake glasses.

"Andy, these aren't Grandma Lupinski's wigs from when she had chemo, are they," Ginger asks.

"Nah, they're wigs Goofy and I used to use when we did runs to Alberta." It's not quite the truth. The long wig was one of Grandma Lupinski's she bought and never wore because she died not long after that. The short wig, Andy bought for Goofy to disguise him.

"Why did Goofy move back to Nojack?"

Andy adjusts Ginger's wig while Ginger does Leo's.

"His dad was dying. You didn't know that? That's why he took that job with Murph," Andy says.

"I'd hate to be a fly on that wall. Goofy barely talks, and Murph can't remember what he said five minutes ago. Hopefully, Murph will take Mouse on and Goofy can return to the llamas."

Leo, puzzled, looks at Andy.

"Goofy is the llama whisperer. They worship him. He's good with plants too. Okay, you should have enough food to get you to Nojack. Don't stop anywhere if you don't have to. Piss in the bushes," Andy says. "Set an alarm for sunrise to remind you to turn off the headlights. They attract attention in daylight. The map shows the side roads to use until sunrise, then hit the highway. It'll be busy and you'll attract less attention there. You meet me at the old bottle depot next to Murph's junkyard."

"I got it, Andy, I wrote it all down last night," Ginger says.

Andy hugs her and Leo. "Okay, Godspeed and good luck. I'll see you soon."

He watches them leave through the back, in Goofy's truck, until a dot on the horizon, feeling a "great swell of love and fear," as Ginger had described it the night before, that irrepressible feeling she had whenever she'd looked at Leo, since the day he was born. Andy described it as "a goldfish wriggling in her heart," and Ginger said, yeah, a goldfish with a razor blade in its teeth.

She had felt love and fear for her husband Randy too, but in that case, she feared him more than she feared for him. With Leo, her fear for him in this world often turned to nightmares, night sweats, panic attacks, especially since Randy "cleaned up," found Jesus, and got custody.

Now they're gone, and he feels a palpable absence of warmth. Goofy's cousins Elmo and Red are due in an hour to housesit the joint. They have no other family now aside from Goofy, and are happy to be able to spend Christmas at the grow op, with the llamas, a full larder, a tree and trimmings, sat TV, and all the weed they can smoke. Andy always makes them a good meal before he leaves and packs his own lunch: cold chicken, fruit salad, bread, cheese, sausages, Coca Colas.

Andy has plans for this Christmas, a big surprise of his own.

# 13

## CHRISTMAS EVE PARTY MENU:

Scallops wrapped in bacon

Pineapple wrapped in bacon

Dates wrapped in bacon

Devilled eggs

Cheese stuffed celery

Radish roses — Lisa

Pickle & sausage platter — Lisa

Cheese & cracker platter — Lisa

Veggies and dip — Lisa

Seafood platter — Rhonda and Mel

Coconut shrimp — Rhonda and Mel

Swedish meatballs — Eddie and Angie

Jamaican Patties — Sherry and Norm

Mini pierogis

Mini quiches

Chicken-drumettes

Baked Potato skins

Stuffed mushrooms

Bread basket

Iced Shortbread

Bacon Fat Gingerbread

Pumpkin tarts

Fruit cake

After Eights

Nuts, chocolates, candy canes

This year, the money has been good and it's a feast, the same thing more or less as other feast years, but now Irma bakes more than she fries and she gets the whole wheat dinner rolls. Lisa has most of her contribution from Safeway this year—she's had no time for anything but wrangling her father home, and anyway, she's of the opinion that women do way too much work over the holidays, even in this day and age. All the same, there are a few things she does, in memory of her late mother.

Both food fridges are full of food, and the bar is stocked with booze and mixers. Out in the garage the beer fridge is full, with cases of two-fours stacked nearby for replenishment, and a big bowl of rolled joints and cigarettes. This is the smoking room.

While Slim sits in a chair drinking a disguised near-beer and finding fault, Lisa and Mouse string garland around the tree, a real tree, filling the place with the smell of pine.

On a nearby bookshelf, Irma has set up her annual Christmas village made up of individual collectible ceramic pieces made by Glassco, woodland creatures, elves, fairies, trees, a skating pond, houses and shops, chapels, all snowy and opalescent. There it was, Mouse thinks, the first throb of Christmas spirit. Hadn't felt it in a while. He tried to describe the feeling to himself, as Dr. Lobo advised. Wonder, he thought. Hope.

"You okay, Mousie?" Lisa says. Denny's words about Mouse at Elk Woods still ring in her ears.

"Yeah."

"Just lost in thought, eh?" She has tears in her eyes, and wraps him up in a big hug. "Best Christmas present is having you back."

"You're squeezing. Me. Too. Hard. Lisa," Mouse says, a bit winded from her embrace, so the words squeak out. Everyone laughs.

"What's so funny?" Norm pokes his head in. "I brought the Jamaican patties, the macaroni salad, and a two-four of Pilsner."

"Thanks, Norm. We're going to fire up a big jay in the garage, want to join?"

"Can't Leese. I have to pick up Sherry at the hospital then we have to get her kid from her parents. We'll see you around six. Sayonara!"

Presents are under the tree, a huge, shiny pile this year. The long buffet is set up in the basement, with hot station and cold station. At four, the first guests arrive, Lisa and Gord's Aunt Ellen who has been watching Lisa's kids. The kids want to open presents now.

"After the party," Lisa says. "Friend presents tonight, family tomorrow. Go give your Grandpa Slim a kiss and then Auntie Irma needs you to put the last ornaments on the tree."

Rhonda and Mel come with Eddie and Angie Redfeather, who has a message from Ginger and Andy Why.

"They'll be in Nojack around 8," Angie says, taking a near beer from Gord. Then she outlines the plan.

Gord makes a suggestion.

"That's brilliant, Gord," Eddie says, clinking his bottle to Gord's. "Two birds, one stone."

Reminds Lisa of the robberies, the way they happened, the ideas, the obstacles, the solutions, and Gord's "systems." How it started as a dark joke during the 1980s recession, then a game, where they got together and jokingly plotted how to rob the Bank of Nova Scotia, the really nice one in Collinedore, a wealthy lakeside town which brought in big tourist money in the summer months. Eventually, with all the bugs worked out, they could see no reason not to knock it over, not during a recession with the bills piling up and the banks, ahem, threatening to foreclose on the houses of their parents.

"Can you do the radish roses?" Irma asks, and Lisa, wrenched back into the moment, takes the Tupperware container of radishes and a thin paring knife. The radishes are traditional from Lisa and Gord's childhood Christmases. The ends are cut off, and then the red skin peeled down but not off, in strips around the white center, then soaked in chilled water, which opens them up like flowers. Every Christmas Lisa did this, along with the carrot curls, and retrieving her father from whatever shack, bar, or jail he might have been in.

In the upstairs living room, Slim is telling the kids about his childhood and Christmases, and Irma turns up the radio to drown him out, or at least mute him, with Christmas carols. Lisa sings along softly. Another tradition: Every Christmas Eve, before the kids go home or crash in sleeping bags in the living room, Norm plays the piano and Lisa sings, solo, a carol. She has a voice, that girl, like an angel and a devil. Not just Irma's opinion but that of a sport fisherman who wandered into the Klondiker on karaoke night, and happened to be a music exec from Toronto.  He said she had a few minor weaknesses, but nothing a good voice coach couldn't handle. He'd like to work with her.

She had her shot, and she walked away from it, brooking no talk of "what might have been," so bad had been her brief experience in the music biz. Now, she's our secret star, Irma thinks. Or one of them.

"Lisa, did you know Goofy paints? Like, he's an artist?"

"Yeah, he made those cast iron garden sculptures two Christmases ago."

"Did everyone know but me?"

"Probably not. I only know because Murph mentioned Goofy spent his spare time welding metal scrap into statues. Goofy would never say anything. He's so autistic."

"Goofy's autistic? Hmm. That makes sense."

"Well, he's somewhere on that spectrum," Lisa says. "Think about it."

Slim is excited about something. His voice cuts through the radio carols. "It's not a lie! One Christmas all we had was squirrel stew and turnips for Christmas dinner, for ten of us, but my mother had saved up enough flour, sugar, and butter to give us each one perfect cookie."

Irma and Lisa look at each other, and their hearts soften. It's not a lie. Slim had it tough, really tough, and his dad was a monster.

"You know, Slim was much better than his father," Irma says.

Lisa nods.  "A vast improvement. He never ever hit Mom once, or us except for a swat on the ass here and there."

"And he didn't drink really until after your mom left him, except for cherry brandy on holidays."

"Oh Jesus, you don't have any around, do you?"

"Hell no. I want a nice Christmas, Lisa. We're feeding him near-beer in Labatt's bottles."

"Gord told me."

"Yeah. He says, they have a placebo effect. Slim thinks he's drunk when really he's just comfortable and tired. But he doesn't get as belligerent."

"One Christmas Dad's dad was broke, as usual, and came home drunk on stump whiskey, in a rage, told the kids there'd be no Christmas because they'd been so bad that year, Santa wasn't coming," Lisa says. "Grandma went to town and begged a Christmas charity basket from the Anglican Church and made a card that said it was from Santa. Grandpa was furious."

"I know. Slim's third worst Christmas."

"I'll say this for Dad, he and Mom always gave us the best possible Christmas they could."

They look at each other again with melting eyes.

Then Slim again, to the impressionable children: "It's not a lie! Back then, for poor people like us, saving up that much sugar alone to make cookies for ten people, was hard. Not like today. She sacrificed for her husband and kids. My Dad was king of the castle. You girls here, that's how you need to be, like my mom. Not this women's lib bull… shoes—"

"That piece of shit. I love how he's polite enough to say bullshoes in front of the kids while he tries to grind his axe against my dead mother and spread his misogynist message."

"Just when you start to warm up to Slim, he sticks a fork in your eye."

"I've had enough." Lisa starts to get up but Irma grabs her arm and sits her back down.

"Let me."

Lisa nods. Irma is better with Slim.

"Men and women are different, and men only marry women, and women are subjective to men, it's the Bible. Hey look at me ya little yard apes! Stop looking at your hand robots. Those hand robots are turning you into robots—That's what Christmas is about ya know, the Bible."

Irma is happy to see that the kids all look to her for rescue from crazy grandpa. They're too smart for this crap.

"Hey Rip Van Winkle. Wake up. It's the 21st century. Those are phones, not 'hand robots,' and since you're talking about the Bible, Pop, I know you'll be going to midnight mass tonight with Gord and Lisa. Do you want another beer?"

"Not right now. I'm starting to feel these. I don't want to fall asleep before the food."

"Or midnight mass."

"Right."

"Okay. Turn the TV back on, kids," Irma says, taking in the relieved smiles of the kids.

# 14

# HARK THE HERALD—HOLY CRAP

They're in the car, singing Christmas carols along with the radio, when Ginger sees the flashing red lights in her rear view mirror.

"Holy crap," she says.

It's not just one car. It looks like three, three flashing red lights, three sirens, zooming up behind her.

But how did they spot her? Here in disguise, in a different vehicle. Andy Why wouldn't sell her out. What gave them away? Who tipped off the cops?

This is it. She has to stop. She's not about to take the cops on a dangerous chase with her son in the car.

She pulls over into the shoulder.

"The jig is up," she says to Leo. "I'm sorry, sweetie."

Leo starts to cry. "They're going to take me away  and put you in jail—
"

The two police cars zoom up beside them.

And zoom past, followed by an ambulance.

The death-cold feeling of dread that has gripped Ginger evaporates.

"They weren't after us!" Leo exults. "Oh, but it must be an accident, two cop cars and an ambulance, probably a bad one, eh. Those folks' Christmas is ruined. That's so sad."

"Yeah," Ginger says, and her heart swells again. Leo's relief is immediately tinged with concern for the stranger/s who need the ambulance. Leo didn't need CLOG's fake Christianity. He had a natural Christian spirit, always, this kid.

"Like Norm says, everyone has some cloud over their Christmas forever. Are there any sandwiches left in the cooler, Leo? We should eat so we don't have to stop until we meet up with Andy."

# 15

# THE CLOUD OVER CHRISTMAS

Officially, Sherry's shift ends at 5pm, but today the last two hours, barring a disaster, would be given over to a party for the patients and staff. No elective surgeries were scheduled at the county hospital over the holidays, so it was all chronic patients and emergencies.

Things could change quickly though, a Christmas tree fire, choking children, food poisoning, drunk drivers. Already, that morning, they'd had a fatality who was DOA, and two ODs, who survived. Sherry would spend the entire holiday season on call, just in case.

"So you can't really relax during the holidays, can you?" Norm had said to her at this same party, a year earlier. "You have to always have your, whatever, antennae up in case of a big accident."

She liked that he picked up on that, and other things. That he noticed she wore a pale lilac colored coat when she left for the day, so when he came to ask her out on their first date he brought flowers and had the florist wrap them in that same color.

He found it almost unbearably sad, people and their families having to spend Christmas in the hospital, for some their last Christmas. Even sadder were those people in the hospital with few or no visitors. Norm joined in the festivities, at this same party the year before, paying special attention to those alone. Despite her misgivings about her former patient, this was when she fell in love with Norm.

This year he's entertaining two old guys who didn't know each other before today, as they resided in different wards, but have a lot in common.

"They were both in Korea at the same time, in the war, even stationed at the same big base for a while, and didn't know each other."

"I am so feeling it now," Sherry says.

"What?"

"The Christmas spirit."

Just then, the hospital's sliding doors open. The cops are there with weeping family members of the day's fatality, come up from Red Deer to identify the body, and Sherry's spirit falters.

"Their Christmas is ruined forever," Norm says softly. "It will always have a cloud over it."

"I'm sure everyone's Christmas has a cloud over it for some reason."

"What is your cloud?"

"That last Christmas with my first husband, before we told Pinky we were getting a divorce. Keeping that secret so as not to ruin her holiday… and from my parents, so as not to ruin theirs.  And of course, it came out in a hundred different ways and culminated with a screaming fight in the parking lot outside of Gran' Market in Edmonton. Oh, and the first Christmas without my grandmother. What's your cloud?"

"Probably when I was eight and my mom was in the hospital giving birth to my brother Charlie and my dad was in the can for illegal deer hunting and resisting arrest. Split us all up, put us in foster homes, eh?

The family I was with, they were just doing a good deed at Christmas to make themselves feel good. Ya know?"

"Yeah."

"I felt like the pet monkey or something. My older sister Lil got one of those families that take in a lot of kids for the bucks, just warehouse them until child services moves them along. But we all found pretty good homes after. The next place I went was with this great old lady, Grandma Lupinski. I was with her when my mom died in the hospital. My dad was still in jail so I stayed with her for four years, had great Christmases with her. She got me into school, which I loved—"

"Because your father didn't believe in school."

"Am I repeating myself? Stop me if I am."

"No, trying to get the timeline clear. You were eight when you started school?"

"I was nine by then."

"And you quit in ninth grade to go work for your father. How old were you?"

"Thirteen, almost fourteen."

"You did nine grades in five years."

"Four. I was out a year with polio—"

"Polio! You never mentioned that."

"Yeah, because I'd never gone to school, I didn't get the vaccinations like other kids. It was a mild case but I was wiped out for a long time. That's why three of the toes on my left foot are shorter than the others."

"Then your dad made you quit school?"

"He needed me to work in the mill. My brothers and sisters washed their hands of him, they lived with new families and went on to other lives, so did I, but he had nobody."

"Jesus."

"That's life, you know. Hey, look where I ended up. I can't complain." He squeezes her arm gently with affection. "Were you here in 1982?"

"No, we were still in Edmonton. But I remember the recession."

"Yeah, six weeks before Christmas 1982 Glassco laid off a bunch of people, just after the last orders went out. That was a bad Christmas all around."

"The year before the bank robberies. When am I going to get the whole story there, Norm?"

"Yeah, listen, Lisa is going to try to tell you all about it. She tells it best. "

"I can't wait."

Sherry goes into her parents' house alone to pick up Pinky, while Norm waits in the car. It's easier that way, if he's not subjected to her father's polite disdain tonight. Of course she understands, how hard they had to work to get to college, to emigrate, to start new in a strange frozen country. Why would anyone not get all the education they could in a place like Canada, where it was so easy?

Of course, they blamed her for the failure of her first marriage. They loved her ex. It didn't matter that she had put her dreams of being a doctor on hold to become a nurse and support him through med school. And her ex claimed to be a "feminist" too. Yeah, a feminist until it impinged in any way on his life. A feminist as long as she did the housework and he was more successful and in control than she was. As long as she was faithful to him. His fidelity was different, he was a man, and from the beginning he had triangulated her with other women and gaslit her about it, to ensure his sexual freedom while controlling her and keeping her off balance to the point of a breakdown that put her in bed and on disability for months.

She would wish she'd never met her ex but then she wouldn't have her daughter Pinky, who sits in the backseat, reviewing video on her phone while talking to Norm at the same time. Pinky might become a doctor, or a scientist, as her grandparents wanted, or a filmmaker, as Pinky wanted. Norm and Pinky got along like old friends, and they were happy as a family now. The ex, that cloud had lifted with Norm, but would always be there, gathering in a back corner like a dark, bearding fungus of regret and grief to descend again when her guard was down.

"Goofy, real name Joey Minot, doesn't talk much, if at all, it's nothing personal."

Norm was cluing Pinky in on some of the people she was going to meet at the party.

"He's autistic I think," Sherry says.

"Why do they call him Goofy?"

"Because of his looks," Norm says.

Sherry protests. "He's very nice looking!"

"Yeah, but he has that kinda hangdog, jowly thing, like the Disney cartoon character, Goofy. I woulda called him Bogart, like Humphrey? But we already knew a guy with that nickname from bogarting joi— uh—"

"I know what bogarting is, Norm," Pinky says.

Norm and Sherry together: "How?"

"I don't smoke marijuana, but I don't live under a rock in a cave either."

"Of course."

"When did you give each other nicknames?" Pinky says.

"At different times, for different reasons, like code names so—"

At this, Sherry shoots him a look. She thinks he might blurt out something about the banks.

"So teachers and parents wouldn't know who we were talking about. And everyone got to veto their nickname. Mine was Drip because I had a recurring post-nasal drip for a couple of years, but a girl I liked heard one of the guys calling me that and she got the wrong idea so I went back to Norm."

"Drip!" Pinky and Sherry together.

"Too much information? Anyway, Goofy will be coming with Murph, who owns the junkyard. Goofy works for him. Or did. He's quitting."

"That has to be difficult, Joey hardly talks, and Murph?" Sherry says.

"Why, Mom?"

"Murph has a problem, well, I'll let you see for yourself. When you meet him, ask him what he thinks of universal health care."

Sherry and Norm laugh.

"Why is that funny?"

"It is and it isn't. You'll see Pinky."

Pinky rolls her eyes. Some private joke among the Olds apparently.

# 16

## MURPH AND GOOFY

Some might find it odd that, though he isn't very social, Goofy always arrives early for the Christmas Eve party, and leaves late. Old Murph comes with Goofy, who comes in, bearing presents. When he puts them down, Mouse walks in.

"Goofy!"

He grabs Goofy and gives him a big hug.

"Should we open them now?" Irma asks, and Goofy nods. "Let's go down to the rec room."

"I'll get you guys plates," Lisa says.

"What do you want to drink?" Gord asks.

They hustle Murph and Goofy downstairs to keep Murph and Slim apart as long as possible, and open Goofy's gifts down there.

Irma opens their box first, extracting what looks like a wasp nest, but in rainbow colors.

"Is that a wasp nest?" Gord says. Goofy nods. "How did you get it to be in all these colors?"

"He puts out different colors of paper mush and the wasps use it in their nests," Murph says. "It's a lampshade. He covered it in a clear, fire-resistant polymer."

"Wow. It's a lampshade, eh?"

Lisa has one too.

"So beautiful, Goofy!"

They all hug Goofy. He blushes. He opens their presents, an art box and chocolates from Mouse, a Visa gift card and hand knitted socks from Irma and Gord, a Harley toque and gloves from Lisa.

"Hey, where are you guys?" It's Norm, calling from the back door vestibule.

"Down here, Norm," Lisa says.

On the way downstairs, they meet Irma, going the opposite direction to check on Slim and keep him upstairs, due to the bad blood between Murph and Slim. Mouse comes down afterwards with beer for Murph and Goofy. Nobody knows what the beef is about exactly, something about Slim's ex-wife, Gord and Lisa's late mother, something about some business deals then a lot of insults, Murph just repeating the same things over and over, Slim getting madder and more profane until they came to blows unless someone got between them.

"Hey Goofy, Hey Murph," Norm says." You remember my wife Sherry?"

Goofy nods and smiles.

"Sherry, yeah, you're black," Murph says.

Murph says the same thing every time he sees her. Sherry is always tempted to say with surprise, "I am? Wow. Excellent." She doesn't.

"And this is Sherry's daughter Pinky. Pinky's doing some research and has a question for you."

"Yeah? What is it?" Murph says.

Pinky clears her throat. "What do you think of universal health care?"

"It's bullshit. I got hit in the back of the head with a meat hook when I was a kid, and my dad cured it with a bread poultice. We didn't need no universal health care."

As instructed beforehand, Pinky asks the same question again.

"It's bullshit. I got hit in the back of the head with a meat hook when I was a kid, and my dad cured it with a bread poultice. We didn't need no universal health care."

"Thank you," Pinky says.

"We're going to go upstairs and help Irma," Sherry says and explains to Pinky on the way, "Murph has a problem with short term memory."

"Probably that meat hook to the back of the head."

"Got a job for you, Murph, Goofy. Your job is to answer the doorbell, okay?" Gord says.

"Sure."

Gord smiles. If the cops come looking for Ginger, Murph and Goofy will distract them and frustrate them long enough to hide Ginger and Leo. Murph hated cops. Two birds one stone, deflect the PoPo and keep Murph busy. Even if they came when Ginger and Leo were there, Murph wouldn't tell them. He'd just say the same nothing over and over.

"And I hear you're leaving the junkyard, Goofy. That means you're going to need someone to work for you, Murph."

Mouse has been sitting quietly.

"Mouse needs a job."

Murph looks at him. "Well, maybe so. I need someone, eh? Goofy's leaving to get married."

That was easier than Mouse expected. Gord was right to let him handle it with Murph. Murph might forget for a while until he got used to seeing Mouse around, but Mouse could deal with it, with Gord's help.

"You're getting married,Goofy?" Norm says.

Goofy blushes and nods.

"Well who is she?"

Goofy blushes harder.

# 17

# ANDY WHY

After Andy drops his load of weed at a medical processing plant in Edson, he heads to Murph's junkyard, with just one stop, at the Lucky Dollar to refill his thermos with coffee. The waitress is talking to some Mounties, and Andy thinks, at first, they might be looking for Ginger because of the Amber alert. But no. It seems there has been some kind of fatality on the road, one dead. Andy panics.

"Was it a lady and a kid?"

One of the Mounties looks at him. "No," she says.

Thank God, Andy thinks, and doesn't want to invite any questions so as soon as he gets his coffee he bolts out the door, touching the lucky dollar quickly as he sweeps out.

It's close to 5 p.m. and dark when Andy gets to Murph's. Ginger is not there and he worries but she pulls in a few minutes later, having stopped en route in some bushes so Leo could pee.

Here Ginger drops Goofy's grandfather's truck then she and Leo get in Andy's van.

"Off to Gord and Irma's?"

"Let's go," Leo says. He's excited, and so excited he looks like he might pop in a blizzard of glitter confetti, like at one of those gender reveal parties.

# 18

## PINKY

"Hey Pinky," Lisa says. "What are ya doing?"

"I'm making a video with my phone to send everyone later."

Angie Redfeather is passing, not a hat exactly, but a red velvet Christmas stocking to raise money for Ginger's "Christmas present."

"Are you buying something or just giving her money?" Pinky asks.

"Money. Guys! We take checks. If you don't have a check, we take cash. No cash, we'll take an IOU and hound you to pay until we get it. Eddie's going to match every cent."

"Turn off the camera, please, Pinky," Lisa says.

She does.

"Where's your mom? Sherry, over here."

"What's up, Lisa?"

"Does she know about Ginger?"

"Oh, a bit."

"Ginger's bringing her son from BC and there's an Amber alert. I saw it on my phone," Pinky says.

"Well, if it comes up, none of you know anything about it," Lisa says. "Angie knows this great family lawyer in Vancouver who also has an office in Kelowna. He's a bit flashy but very good, she says. We're raising money to pay him."

"I think Ginger wins in the court of public opinion," Pinky says. "A mom taking her son so he doesn't miss Christmas? Risking it all to give her son Christmas? It could go viral if properly positioned. Here, Lisa. I'm sending you my e-card with my social media info. Give it to the lawyer and have him contact me to discuss his social media strategy. Can I turn on the camera now, if I'm careful about the Ginger stuff?"

"Sure," Lisa says. Her phone dings with Pinky's e-card.

She and Sherry wait until Pinky is in the next room before they turn to each other and laugh.

"Wait, wasn't she 15 at my birthday party, July fourth? How did she turn 30 so fast," Lisa says. "'Social media strategy.'"

"Oh she means it," Sherry says. "And she knows what she's talking about."

"Kids today."

"Norm says you'll tell me about the bank... jobs tonight?"

"Tonight? I doubt we'll have time tonight, if we make it through tonight. Gord and I always do midnight mass on Christmas Eve, in honour of our mom. You're doing the Jamaican thing tomorrow?"

"Yeah."

"How about Boxing Day? We do a grownups day in the garage with karaoke and leftovers."

"That's perfect," Sherry says. "Pinky's with her dad and her stepmom."

"You think he's pulling the same shit on the second wife?"

"I don't know. Probably. But new wife thinks he's wonderful and I'm the crazy witch. Maybe he doesn't have to triangulate her with any other woman because he has the evil ex-wife to control her."

Pinky has found Slim.

"Oh look another pipsqueak following her hand robot, and this one's black."

"I'm making a video."

"Not of me," Slim says.

So Pinky turns the camera away to film the tree and various kids hamming it up around it. She likes the details, the layers of tradition, ornaments marked with years past, 1967, 1974, 1982 and so on. Pinky's dad and stepmom will have a beautiful tree in white, red and gold, the ornaments all matching, and it will be beautiful. But nothing beats a tree like this, old delicate blown glass birds and bells mixed with the popcorn and cranberry garland, the Lucky Oilers ornament, the old stars of wood and gold-sprayed pasta made by children years ago. For a moment, Pinky feels like she's five again, in front of one of her grandmother's Jamaican Blue Mountain pines.

Then she's 15-going-on-30 again, wandering the party, filming the Olds and their various conversations.

Rhonda: Glenn has his dream job, he runs a golf course for rich assholes on Van island. He lives in this cool house on the grounds, view of the sea, with a woman he met in an astronomy forum and they're doing well I think.

Angie: Mikey got her big rig license; she's hauling dry goods...

Eddie: Yeah, I remember going fishing with Slim and Murph.

Gord:  Yeah, to the local fish farm with wire cutters, six big black garbage bags and a net.

Eddie: Ate trout for a year. Can't look at it now.

# 19

# GINGER AND LEO

Mouse is out in the garage, getting beer when Andy, Ginger, and Leo arrive through the back door of the garage.

"Merry Christmas!" He shouts.

"Sshh, Mousie." Ginger gives him a big hug, then Leo. "Sooo good to see you, you son of a bee. We need to get inside. See you in there."

The garage has a small cellar which leads underground to the house. It was there when Gord and Irma moved in, and nobody knows why except maybe to avoid going out in the bitter Wesaskawa winds in January and February. This is their route in to avoid being seen by any nosy neighbors, and it has come in handy many times.

Irma is waiting by the basement door inside, alerted by a coded text from Andy Why. A crowd gathers and when Ginger and Leo walk in they are enveloped by hug after hug.

Mouse is still in the garage when he sees Officers DiMara and Oleanik walk up the back sidewalk through the frost-framed window in the garage. He sends Irma an urgent text so they can hustle Ginger and Leo into the tunnel behind the secret door, and push a shelving unit of tools in front of it.

Irma texts back, "Thanks. A-OK."

The very sight of the cops made Mouse jittery, an old habit, and he has decided to wait it out here.

He takes a near beer out of the old fridge, a white Frigidaire. Gord has left the CD player on with Christmas carols on a loop, and put a box of cigarettes in the garage with fireplace matches and an Oilers lighter on an old coffee table from the 1960s with fake wood finish and stiletto legs. Mouse only likes an occasional cigarette but he feels like one now. He opens his near beer, sits down in an old La-Z-Boy by the coffee table and fires up a Player's, smoking as he sings along to Ye Merry Gentlemen.

"Mouse?"

No, it can't be.

"Mouse?"

He looks around, sees no one to go with the loud whisper.

"Yeah," he says.

"You're alone?"

"Yeah. Tammy?"

She pops her head out from behind an old piano.

"Oh my God, Tam, what happened to you?"

Her face is bruised and scraped and bloody, blood all over her clothes, and she's cradling an arm. She's been crying.

"It's bad," she says.

# 20

# MAKE THE RIGHT CHOICE, MOUSE

When the doorbell rings, Goofy takes Murph up to answer Officers DiMara and Oleanik.

But DiMara and Oleanik are not looking for Ginger.

"Have you seen Tammy," DiMara asks. "We believe she may be here."

"Who?" Murph says.

Goofy goes to get Irma.

"Get Mouse," she says. "He's in the garage."

When Goofy opens the garage door, Tammy ducks down behind the piano, and Mouse is startled, and looks it.

"Oh, Goofy."

"Irma. Um. Wants you. Now."

Mouse doesn't have to ask if it's important. Goofy spat out each word in record time.

"Okay, you and I can go in together, Goofy," he says, and they leave Tammy alone, and go out to face the police.

"Mouse, have you heard from Tammy? Do you know where she is," DiMara asks.

Mouse freezes.

"Mouse, she killed a man. Don't get into any more trouble for her," Irma says.

"Make the right choice, Mouse," says Gord.

And he does. "She's in the garage, hiding behind the piano. What happened?"

"Is she armed?"

"Not now."

DiMara nods at Oleanik, and he goes into the garage.

The crowd is gathered in the back porch foyer, spilling into the kitchen. Pinky discreetly films with her phone. Norm and Sherry open a kitchen window to hear.

"Found a man's body earlier today, stabbed in the heart on a logging road off the Yellowhead. Ran the prints on the knife and she came up right away. He's a truck driver named Brad Easton—"

Sherry whispers to Norm. "Oh my God, that's the fatality we had in ER today."

"We also got some security video froma truck stop, Tammy leaving with Easton."

"Tammy wouldn't kill anyone," Mouse says, "Except in self-defense."

"Well, Mouse, his money and credit cards were missing. So it could be a robbery—"

# 21

# REAL TROUBLE

Somewhere after Entwistle, Tammy starts to think she's in real trouble. First the guy grabs her purse from her side, says it's in his way, and throws it in the back, removing her access to her phone and any weapon she may have in there. Is she being too suspicious? Maybe. But then he turns to look out his side mirror and she sees the jagged scar on the back of his neck, faded and mostly grown over. The guy who killed Cindy Crowchild, he had a scar there.

Lots of people have scars but when he turns down a small, empty logging road, surrounded by dense forest and bush, and tells her it's a shortcut, she knows. This is no shortcut.

He pulls into a stand of trees.

"I need to piss. How about—?" He says.

Before he can finish his sentence, Tammy has a knife out of her belt and in his chest. It doesn't kill him right away, the knife jams in a rib. She puts a boot in his stomach to pin him to the driver side door, as he hits and scratches, and to give her some leverage to remove the knife, so she can jam it in again, harder, and straight to the heart.

There's blood everywhere, on the seat, the dashboard, the pine tree deodorizer hanging off the mirror.   He gurgles blood from his mouth.

Is he dead? No pulse. She opens his door and pushes his body out on the snowy road. Covered in blood as she is, there's no hope of trying to hitch another ride. She'll have to drive this behemoth to Nojack.

She feels like she's on meth or crack, even though she's completely sober. Wired up, scared, but at the same time feeling something, oddly, good. She drives to a stand of trees near Irma and Gord's, and waits there until night, when she sneaks into their garage. She's there all night and the next day, hiding when Gord and Irma fill the fridge in the morning, when Lisa comes out to get near beer.

# 22

# A GODDAMN CHRISTMAS MIRACLE

Officer DiMara gets an alert. She looks at her phone. "The chief," she says, and steps away to talk to him, walking towards the garage before stopping suddenly.

"WHAT? Holy shit." She clicks off. "They finished running all the prints on the knife, and the victim's name is not Brad Easton."

"What? Who is he?" Oleanik says.

"Eugene Svunya," DiMara says. "That's his real name. His prints link him to a murder of a young woman in Northern California in 2001, which appears to be linked to many more. She tore off part of his glove with her teeth, leaving the fingerprint exposed."

"What was her name," Tammy asks.

"Brandi Walchuk. Uh, why?"

"I want to know who she was so I can pray for her and thank her spirit for that." Then she bursts into tears.

Tammy now sits in one of the old armchairs in the garage with DiMara, Oleanik, Mouse, Gord, Irma and Sherry, who is tending Tammy with the house first aid kit.

Irma gives her a Coca-Cola and Gord gives her a cigarette.

"They're going to be doing the DNA profile and run that too. He's suspected in a string of murders up and down the US West coast."

"And Canada. My friend, Cindy Crowchild. Maybe he's the guy who killed her."

"Whoa," Gord says. "Well, even if he wasn't, you and Brandi did something for her too, Tammy. If there's a heaven, she's thanking you from it."

Oleanik speaks. "We should take Tammy to hospital first, get those bruises and that arm looked at, then to the station."

As DiMara walks away she says, "We'll be back, about that other matter. You know what I'm talking about."

"We'll be back on December 27th at 5pm," Oleanik says, and winks. "December 27th, 5pm."

"Understood," Irma says.

"Merry Christmas, guys," Gord says.

As the cops take Tammy away, Whiskey drives up and staggers out of his car.

"Tammy!" He shouts, just before he trips and lands on his face.

"Are you drunk, Whiskey?" DiMara says. "You drove drunk here? Cuff him. We'll take him with us."

"Let's go back inside," Irma says, hunching into herself from the cold.

"Holy fuck, Tammy killed a serial killer."

"I read a book about those murders. There were at least seven," Irma says.

"That was the fatality at Sherry's hospital today," Norm said. "Say a prayer for that guy's family at mass tonight. We saw them at the ER today. Imagine, learning your dad is dead, and then learning he's a serial killer."

All this time, Ginger and Leo have been huddled behind the secret door in the basement to the garage. Irma frees them now.

"You're off the hook until 5pm December 27th. DiMara and Oleanik did you a good one, and so did Tammy," Irma tells Ginger.

"Tammy?"

"Tammy saved Christmas, saved herself, and saved you and Leo."

"Who knows how many future victims saved. Think of those women, sittin' at home this Christmas eve, who have no idea that Tammy has saved their lives," Gord says.

While Irma fills Ginger in on what she considers a goddamn Christmas miracle, Lisa sits down with Mouse in the kitchen. She has been bothered since her ex-boyfriend Denny told her about meeting Mouse on the way to Elk Woods. It's been hard not telling Irma, but Irma will never get it out of her mind. She had been in fits with anxiety when Mouse went away.

So Lisa has to keep this to herself: that the crazy guy who insisted on being called Mr. Sinatra and bit off the end of Mouse's finger was Mouse himself. Someone told him he could get his own cell if he did something crazy and he panicked.

Jesus Christ.

"How are you doing, Mousie?"

"I dunno. So much to think about. I got a doctor in Edmonton I'm s'posed to call in the new year to talk to. He's a friend of Dr. Lobo."

"He could help. And you can always talk to me. How do you feel about Tammy? Are you wanting to get back together with her now?"

"No. When I saw her, I didn't feel good, Leese. I felt like a big hand was squeezing me, like, anxiety, eh, and—and I didn't feel good about myself in her eyes. Or mine. Does that make sense?"

"Yeah. But it doesn't matter how you look in Tammy's eyes, only in yours. You know you look damned wonderful to us. I'm going to get some food."

"I'll join you."

Andy Why and Goofy had some news, but now is not the time.

Slim, convinced he was drunk from near-beers, has fallen asleep in the living room.

At the kids all change into their pajamas and brush their teeth. It's another of Gord's systems, a gift to their parents. Being in their pajamas has a psychological effect, Gord figures, and makes them sleepier so there's no wrestling kids wired for Christmas into bed when they get home. Just take off their coats and boots and pop them into the sack.

At 11 they turn on the Edmonton local news to see what they have on Tammy. She's the top story, sitting in front of a bouquet of news microphones. Tammy is a big hero, and she seems to be enjoying the attention.

It turns out there's a big reward from a victim's family in the USA, $200,000 and Tammy is going to get it.

What will she do now?

"My boyfriend Whiskey, uh, James, and I are going to start a nail salon and I don't know what else," she says to the microphones.

"Whiskey. Figures," Irma says. "I'm glad Tammy's okay, but it's so fucking unfair that Tammy's now rich, and Mouse went to jail for her."

"And Whiskey won the lotto. That still ticks me off," Lisa says. "Mousie, you're married to Tammy, you could get a divorce finally and take some of that money."

"Divorce yes," he says. "But I don't want her money."

"You do. We'll talk about it later," Lisa says.

It occurs to Irma that Tammy has also saved Mouse, saved Mouse from Tammy herself.

"We gotta get ready to go Lisa, if we're going to make midnight mass."

"Coming, Gord." No Christmas Carol sung by Lisa tonight for the kids, but she'll sing for the angels at mass.

Another Christmas Eve party breaks up, tipsy stragglers, designated drivers and children, leaving behind a detritus of torn wrapping paper and food-smeared plates, and Slim, snoring in the living room.

"Well this was a Christmas for the books," Irma says as she sees them off.

"Merry Fucking Christmas," Norm calls out.

"And to all a good fucking night," Gord adds, pulling Irma close and giving her a big kiss before he heads off to church.


## END BOOK ONE


**To Be Continued.**

Printed in Great Britain
by Amazon